HER LIFELONG DREAM

HER LIFELONG DREAM

•

Judy Kouzel

AVALON BOOKS
NEW YORK

PRINTED IN THE UNITED STATES OF AMERICA
ON ACID-FREE PAPER
BY HADDON CRAFTSMEN, BLOOMSBURG, PENNSYLVANIA

To Ron, Alex, and Susan

Chapter One

Leedy Collins pulled her old, dark green Jeep Wrangler into the closest parking space she could find. She glanced briefly at the white stucco building for a second before she flung open the car door and headed for the entrance. It was a beautiful early fall day in Madison, Wisconsin, but Leedy barely noticed. Her thoughts were a million miles away.

Please approve the loan, please approve the loan, she prayed to herself as she opened the gleaming glass doors and walked into the lobby. But of course they would approve the loan—at long last. Why else would she have received the phone call yesterday?

"Hello, Ms. Collins," the friendly voice on the other end of the line had said. "My name is Greta Spencer and I'm with Bernard & Simmons Savings and Loan. Terry Foster, the loan officer in charge of your case, would like to meet with you to discuss your loan application. Would it be possible to set up a meeting?"

"Absolutely," Leedy had said. She would have driven to

1

the bank right then and there but instead she had to settle for a meeting early the next morning. She could hardly sleep that night. Could all of her hard work finally be paying off?

The enormity of the day weighed heavily on her as she made her way to Suite 10-B, so much so that her knees were shaking and her stomach was churning all the way up to the tenth floor of the office building. She walked down the hallway, her thoughts on the San Francisco culinary institute she had attended and the many years of working for restaurants large and small. From busgirl to hostess to server to chef's assistant, Leedy had done it all. Her resume was a testimony to her qualifications as a capable restaurateur. No doubt about it—she knew the food business inside and out.

"Yes, my restaurant will be a welcome addition in Madison," she whispered, imagining the faceless loan officer who handed her the check. "Yes, I'm an experienced chef and an excellent manager. I'm also a master of organization and . . ."

"May I help you?" a woman from behind a big mahogany desk asked. The nameplate on her desk said the woman's name was 'Greta Spencer, Administrative Supervisor.'

"Um . . . yes. I'm here to see Ms. Terry Foster."

"*Mr.* Foster is taking a telephone call at the moment, Miss . . . ?"

"Oh . . . sorry. I'm Leedy . . . um . . . I'm Carolee Collins. I have a nine o'clock appointment."

"Oh yes," the woman said. "Mr. Foster will be right with you, Ms. Collins. Please have a seat." Leedy sat on a small sofa near an oversized potted plant. She wished the butterflies would stop fluttering in her increasingly agitated stomach. She picked a piece of lint from her skirt and wondered, once again, if the navy blue suit she had chosen made her look professional enough.

"Mr. Foster will see you now," Ms. Spencer said after what seemed like forever. Leedy glanced at the clock on the wall and saw it had only been eight minutes.

"Thank you," she said, flashing Ms. Spencer a confident smile. She took a deep breath and bravely walked into Terry Foster's office.

Of course, just as she stepped into the room, she heard the telephone on his desk begin to ring. "Terry Foster," the man in the charcoal gray suit said, picking up the receiver. He waved her in, giving her a quick smile. "I'll be with you in just a moment," he said, covering the mouthpiece on the telephone.

Leedy looked around the office. It was what she had imagined a banker's office should look like. Formal and dignified with the requisite large wooden desk and leather-upholstered chairs. Mighty nice digs these bankers have, she thought to herself.

"Yes, sir," Terry Foster was saying into the telephone. "We can handle that transaction for you . . . Absolutely. I don't see any problem on our end of the deal . . . I'll have the paperwork ready for you by the close of business today . . ."

She watched him as he spoke. He was younger than what she expected a banker would be. Probably about the same age as she was. He was attractive too. And his voice was nice—deep and smooth as velvet with a slight Southern twang to it. He had the kind of voice Leedy could almost imagine whispering in her ear late at night. Sexy and strong.

She blushed as if Terry Foster could read her thoughts. She didn't ordinarily allow her imagination to run away from her. But the physical attractiveness and youth of the loan officer was something she had not bargained for and she was momentarily caught off-guard. The last thing she needed today was to appear to be distracted. This was, after all, a business meeting.

"Perhaps you should come to my office tomorrow morning to talk about it," Terry Foster was saying to the caller. "I'm certain we can hammer out all the details . . . Good. I'll see you at nine-thirty tomorrow morning. . . . Absolutely. I'm looking forward to it. Say hello to Barbara and the girls for me. See you then . . . Goodbye." He hung up the phone and turned his attention to Leedy. "Is it warm in here?" he asked.

"No," she said. "I don't think so."

"You look a little flushed," he said. "May I offer you something to drink—coffee or a soft drink or maybe a glass of cold water?"

"No," she said, feeling her face redden even further. "I'm fine. Thank you."

"I'm sorry about the phone call. It rings off the hook this time of day," he said, extending his hand. "You must be Ms. Collins. As you may have already concluded, I'm Terry Foster, and I'm the loan officer assigned to your application."

"Mr. Foster," she said, meeting his handshake.

The instant his hand touched hers, Leedy felt a tremble go through her body all the way to her toes. His grip was self-assured and strong, but, at the same time, exciting. "Please call me Terry," he said, pumping her hand.

"Very well . . . Terry," she said, trying to ignore the electricity of his touch. But he was a hard man to ignore. He was tall, at least six foot two, with a mop of brown hair that had a boyish curl to it and a warm smile that flashed perfect white teeth. She instinctively knew he was a runner, despite the business suit. An avid runner herself, she could always recognize another runner's physique.

But what she noticed most about Terry Foster were his eyes. They were the most extraordinary shade of deep blue she had ever seen. The blue eyes, along with the brown curls and the dazzling smile made it difficult for her to remember why she was standing in his office.

Leedy pulled herself together. What *was* she thinking? She was not there to look for a . . . a . . . boyfriend. For Pete's sake, that was the last thing in the world she wanted in her life. A man would only sidetrack her from her ultimate goal. She was there to see about getting a bank loan so she could open her restaurant. And nothing more.

"It's nice to meet you," she said, returning his strong grip with one of her own. "I'm Leedy Collins."

He smiled again, still shaking her hand. It was turning into the longest handshake she had ever known, but she didn't mind. The banker squeezed her hand one last time before he slowly and reluctantly released it. "Please have a seat," he said, pointing to a pair of identical black leather chairs across from his desk.

"Thank you," she said, sitting down. She already missed the feel of his hand touching hers.

"Leedy . . . that's an unusual name," he began. "Your application said your name is Carolee."

"It is," she said. "My mother's name is Edith. My father

called me Lil' Edie when I was a child. It eventually evolved into Leedy. You know—Carolee, Lil' Edie . . . Leedy. Somehow it stuck."

"It is a pretty name—and unique. I like it." His eyes met hers for a moment and she felt her heart jump.

"Thank you," she said, her cheeks beginning to blush once more. She tore her eyes away from his and concentrated on the folder that sat on the desk in front of him. "I . . . um . . . I hope all of my paperwork was in order?"

"Yes," he said, with another radiant smile. "You didn't miss a single detail in your documentation. You're also well-informed on the specific requirements necessary when opening a new restaurant. I can see you know your business, Leedy. I also see that you're an organized thinker."

"Thank you," she said again. She noticed he had called her by her first name. She liked the way it sounded coming from his lips. Like something warm and delicious was tickling his tongue. She watched as his mouth moved, but she was no longer listening to the words he said. His voice was low and sensual and soothing. She was finding it hard to concentrate. "I wonder what it would feel like if he were to kiss me," she thought to herself, and the idea made her feel strangely warm. "Stop!" she ordered herself, digging her fingernails into the palms of her hands.

"I asked you here today so we could discuss your loan application," Terry Foster was saying, pulling her thoughts back to the business at hand. "Can you tell me why it is you wish to open a restaurant?"

"Of course," Leedy said, ignoring the soft stirring that had begun deep inside of her. "It has been my lifelong dream to open a restaurant of my own, Mr. Foster."

"Terry."

"Terry. I've wanted to run my own restaurant ever since I was a child. When I was a little girl, I used to make my parents sit at the dinner table while I took their orders. The first job I ever had was in a fast-food place. As a matter of fact, I've never worked for any other kind of business. My entire career has been with food services. I've been a bus-girl, dishwasher, hostess, server, cook . . ."

"Yes," Terry Foster said. His deep blue eyes scanned her loan application. "I see you attended the Cornwell Institute."

"Yes. It's in California."

"I'm familiar with Cornwell," he said. "It's a highly respected cooking institute. Very impressive."

"Thank you again."

"But you're not currently working as a chef," he noted.

"That's right."

"I see you're the manager of Mr. Hobo's?"

"Yes," Leedy said. Her mouth was dry and her heart was pounding. "I'm sure it looks odd on my resume, Mr. Foster, but I took the job at Mr. Hobo's as a calculated career move. I wanted to learn the workings of the restaurant business from all perspectives—not just the kitchen and dining room. I wanted more insight into the management side of things."

"I see," he said. "Please, call me Terry."

"Terry . . . The head chef at Mr. Hobo's is wonderful. His name is Paul Marcus. I fill in for him from time to time . . . when he's out sick or away on vacation. I love to cook, obviously. But I wanted to work more on the front lines."

"I can't argue with your logic, Leedy. And you've been employed with Mr. Hobo's for how long?"

"It's been six months now," she said. "But I'm a quick study."

"I'm certain of that," Terry Foster said, giving her another one of his winning smiles. "I hear Mr. Hobo's is the place to go in town these days."

"Yes, it is," she said, nodding. "The food is good, and it isn't as pricey as some of the other places in town. It's especially popular with the college students."

"So I've heard." He flipped through the papers on his desk again. "I haven't been there yet, but I plan on going soon."

"You should. Everyone likes it there."

He looked up from the application and smiled. "And I can tell that Mr. Hobo's is a good place for you to learn the ropes of running a restaurant. But . . ."

"But?"

"But six months is not a lot of time to gain much on-the-job experience, is it?"

"No," she said. "But I've been working in restaurants in one capacity or another since I was fourteen years old, Mr. Foster."

"Terry."

"Terry," she said. "I know the business inside and out."

He was looking at her paperwork and nodding, but Leedy had the sudden sinking feeling that maybe she was not there to learn that her loan was approved after all. "I think it is important that you understand the concept of the restaurant I have in mind," she blurted. She was almost too nervous to speak, but the words came bubbling up out of her. "I want you to get a clear picture of exactly the kind of restaurant I wish to open. It will not be in competition with Mr. Hobo's, if that's what you're worried about."

He looked up at her and studied her carefully. "No. I don't see that as a problem. But I'm listening. Tell me about the restaurant you have in mind."

"Don't get me wrong," she said, looking him in the eye. "I like my job . . . very much so. Mr. Hobo's is a wonderful place. It's well run and the food is delicious. But it isn't the type of restaurant I want to open."

"Oh?"

"No. Not at all. The restaurant I want to open is nothing like Mr. Hobo's."

Terry looked up again from the folder and fixed his dazzling eyes on her. "Well then, by all means, Leedy. Tell me all about your plans."

"The restaurant I'm proposing will be distinctive," she said. "It will be the kind of place that people from all over Wisconsin will come to."

"Is that so? Tell me more."

"Okay. Picture a New England inn, only more upscale and fashionable. My restaurant will be decorated in soft, muted colors with exquisite furnishings. The menu will be small, but the food will be state-of-the-art gourmet cooking from recipes I developed myself. It will have an extensive wine cellar. A restaurant like the one I have in mind would be more than just a place to eat, Mr. Foster. My restaurant will be anything but run-of-the-mill. My restaurant will be the finest eatery in town and an asset to the entire Madison community."

He raised his eyebrows again and Leedy detected a trace of amusement in the expression on his handsome face. "Call me Terry," he said gently.

"Terry," she said, taking a deep breath.

"I confess," the banker said after a long pause. "I had

formulated a picture in my mind of your restaurant as I reviewed your loan application, Leedy, and by the description you just gave me, I realize I was not far off the mark. I think I have a clear idea of the place you have in mind."

Leedy nodded and smiled. Finally, someone with vision!

He continued. "And obviously, you have a great deal of . . . passion for your work. And, personally, I would love to see a restaurant like the one you describe open up in town. As a matter of fact, I would probably be the first person in line on opening day. But . . ."

"But?" she echoed, her heart sinking.

"But you have a few problems that need addressing."

"Problems?"

"Yes," he said. "First of all, you want to open an upscale restaurant . . ."

"What's wrong with opening an upscale restaurant?"

"There is nothing wrong with opening an upscale restaurant, per se. Except this is a college town and the average student is more interested in burgers than gourmet. And there are several upscale restaurants already, some of which are struggling."

"I've been to those restaurants," Leedy said. "I know where their problems lie and I can assure you, Mr. Foster . . . er . . . Terry, I will not make the same mistakes they've made."

"There are also some concerns about the human resources information you provided," he added.

"What sort of concerns?"

"You counted yourself as both the manager and the head chef. How can you do both of those jobs at the same time?"

"As I said before, I know my way around the dining room as well as the kitchen," she said. "Besides, there will be an assistant chef, a hostess, servers, dishwashers and . . ."

"You would still have to work a twenty-hour day to keep up with that pace," he said.

"I could do that," Leedy said.

"I believe you could," he said. "For a time anyway. But . . ."

"But?" The conversation had turned, and things were not going as well as she hoped they would.

"Your financial figures were vague in some areas," the banker said.

"I wanted to keep my budget flexible," she explained. "In case something unexpected came up."

"Something unexpected usually does. But the bank needs specific information, Leedy. For instance, your wine cellar. That's a rather expensive addition, don't you think?"

"Yes," she agreed. "But a well-stocked wine list is essential for a good restaurant."

"I agree. But the figure you have allocated isn't nearly enough to pay for the type of wine cellar you have in mind. Why, one bottle alone could cost more than . . ."

"I plan to start with a modest list and purchase more as the cash flow takes hold." She saw the skeptical expression on his face and grimaced. "Look," she said her voice dropping. "I'm a hard worker and I've been working toward this for my entire adult life. I know I can make it work!"

Terry Foster frowned and put the folder back onto the top of the stack. "I'm sorry, Ms. Collins," he said, looking genuinely apologetic. "Leedy . . . The bank's approval committee couldn't possibly endorse your application for a loan at this time. Perhaps you could try again after . . ."

Leedy's heart sank. "Does this mean that I didn't get the loan?" she asked.

"I'm sorry," he said. "I would be happy to suggest a possible course of action for you to take to better prepare yourself for the future. In fact, I have some ideas that you may wish to consider . . ."

"Ideas?" Leedy was dumbstruck. "What kind of ideas?"

"Well, I would be happy to make a few recommendations for you to follow. I have an eighteen-month plan of action I would like to present, if you have the time . . ."

"Are you saying you asked me to come here to your office so that you could tell me my loan application was *declined*?"

"I know you're disappointed," Terry Foster said. "But this is no reflection on . . ."

A tear spilled down Leedy's cheek and she brushed it away, angry with herself for letting such a thing happen. "But you're the fifth bank I've been to," she said, fighting back the tears. "You were my last hope."

"Please, sit down," he said. "I'd like to talk more about your application." It was a request that caught Leedy off-guard because she did not know she had gotten to her feet, her purse slung over her shoulder and her car keys in her hand.

"Okay," she said simply, and sat back down. Maybe he would now tell her it had all been a terrible mistake—a mix-up with files perhaps—and her loan was approved after all. But the expression of concern on the banker's handsome face told her all she needed to know. This was no mistake.

She barely listened as he spoke, his voice almost a tickle in her ear. She just nodded at him and fought the tears back that threatened to fall at any second. "This isn't to say that we won't consider your application at another time," he was saying.

"I understand," Leedy said and stood up again. Her disappointment was tremendous and she knew that if she didn't leave right away, she was going to burst into tears. "Thank you for seeing me, Mr. Foster. The other banks just sent a letter."

"Bernard & Simmons is not like the other banks," Terry Foster said. "And . . ."

"I'm sorry," she said, forcing herself to smile. "But I have to go."

With that, Leedy turned and fled. The idea of falling apart right in front of a good-looking loan officer was too embarrassing an option to consider. Instead, she dashed from the room, leaving Terry Foster still sitting at his desk, looking bewildered. She almost made it to the elevator before she heard him call out to her. "We'll talk again when you have more time," he said and she nodded.

Thankfully, the elevator doors glided open and she stepped into the box. She rode the crowded elevator down without incident, but it was all she could do to keep from sobbing. Once the doors slid open again, she strode quickly through the lobby until, finally, she pushed open the gleaming glass door that let her out of Bernard & Simmons Savings and Loan. Not even the feel of the warm autumn sunshine on her face made her feel better.

Leedy didn't allow herself to cry until she was finally sheltered in the privacy of her car. Then she couldn't hold back any longer. The tears spilled down her cheeks as she cried. Five minutes later, she was able to wipe her eyes with a crumpled tissue and put her keys in the ignition. She couldn't very well sit in her car and cry all day, but, some-how, she didn't know what else to do with herself. She had arrived there with such high hopes.

Finally, she put her car into gear and headed out of the bank's parking lot. There was nothing else to do but go home. Go home with the knowledge that her dream of own-ing her own restaurant was just as far away as it always had been.

Chapter Two

Leedy went home and allowed herself a good, long cry. Then she remembered Terry Foster's good-looking face and the sound of his sexy voice and cried some more. She trembled with embarrassment every time she thought of the way she had dashed out of his office, almost in tears. He must have thought she was crazy.

When she finished crying, she put on her well-worn running clothes and headed out to the nearby park to run around Lake Benjamin. It was a beautiful day, and the park was full of pleasant people enjoying the sunny autumn morning.

Leedy ran around and around the perimeter of the small lake. Once, twice, three times around. She liked the sound her feet made as they slapped the asphalt pathway and the feel of the sunshine against her cheeks. Four, five, six times around. The back of her shirt was wet from her sweat. Seven, eight, nine, ten times around. Leedy checked her breathing and pressed on. She ran and ran until she lost count of the number of laps. She ran until she thought her lungs would burst. Finally, she slowed and walked the final lap around the lake while her breathing returned to normal. She was tired, but it was a good tired. But not even physical exhaustion could take away the bitter disappointment of that morning.

The image of Terry Foster kept floating back to her, filling her with an ache that left her shaking with frustration. A few more tears spilled down Leedy's cheeks as she finished up the final trip around the lake. She brushed them away impatiently and slowly headed back to her apartment, breathing in the crisp, clean air in an effort to soothe her bruised spirit.

She knew she had to somehow pull herself together before she reported to Mr. Hobo's that afternoon. Friday nights were always the busiest night of the week at the restaurant, especially since classes at the University of Wisconsin had begun again. Her evening would be a busy one, and she had to be on her toes.

Back in her apartment, Leedy took a long bubble bath. She sank into the hot, sweet-smelling water and closed her eyes, trying to forget about her miserable day. But it did no good. Her heart was broken. Her frustration was too profound, her discouragement too great. All she could do was lay in the tub and let her disappointment wash over her.

Leedy finally gave a heavy sigh and pulled out the stopper from the drain with her big toe. The water drained out of the tub slowly . . . much the same way all hope had been drained from her dreams. Leedy contemplated such melodramatic thoughts as she looked up at the ceiling while the water drained. Only when the water was gone did she slowly climb out of the tub and begin to dress for work.

She looked through the steam in the mirror over the sink and examined herself intently. She still looked like the same person she had been that morning, despite her flushed face from the hot bath and the crying binge. She still had the same long, glossy brown hair and the same big chestnut-colored eyes. She applied her make-up carefully, then blew her hair dry. Yes, it was her all right. Same heart-shaped face, same high cheekbones, same dimple on one cheek only (the left).

The restaurant-issued black tuxedo Mr. Hobo's required her to wear fit her tall, athletic build perfectly. In fact, except for the pink cheeks, no one would know to look at her that she had had such a disappointing morning. The image of the loan officer popped into her mind and she felt embarrassed all over again.

Leedy stuck her tongue out at the mirror, found her car keys and purse, and then bounded out the door, angry with herself for thinking of Terry Foster and his stupid blue eyes.

By the time she arrived at Mr. Hobo's fifteen minutes later, she was beginning to feel like her old self again. She was already thinking about the loan application she would submit to another bank. If it had caught the attention of Bernard & Simmons Savings and Loan, maybe it would catch the eye of someone else. She just had to keep trying.

The parking lot was packed, so she knew before she walked in the door that Mr. Hobo's would be in full swing. "What's with the mob scene, Brittany?" Leedy asked the pretty blond waitress who dashed past her.

"There must be something going on at the University," Brittany said with her usual pixie-like smile. "We've been this busy since eleven o'clock and there's no end in sight. How did your meeting at the bank go?"

"Not good," Leedy said. "I'll tell you about it later." She had confided in Brittany about her hopes of opening her own restaurant. It was unusual for her to be so forthright when it came to her dream restaurant. It was an aspiration that was too precious to share, especially with an employee. But there was something about Brittany's sweet personality that told Leedy she could trust her.

They'd hit it off from the moment they first met. As a matter of fact, although they hadn't known each other long, Leedy thought of Brittany as one of her best friends. "Didn't you have something you had to do tonight?" Leedy asked.

"Mark and I are supposed to pick out our china and silver patterns," Brittany said. "My mother wants to tag along, of course. Mark will be here any minute . . . But if you need me to stay and help, I will. I don't mind and I'm sure Mark will understand."

"No way," Leedy said. "You've already put in a long day, Brit. You and Mark have a great time shopping. We can hold down the fort without you."

Brittany was getting married to her long-time boyfriend, Mark Ellis, in less than three months, and she was busy tending to the last-minute details. Pre-wedding stress aside, it was obvious to anyone who met the attractive young couple that there was something special between them.

Leedy was thrilled for Brittany and enjoyed talking with her about every detail of her wedding plans, especially the reception. But there were also times when she envied Brittany too. Her cheeks would redden with shame whenever she had these feelings. She loved Brittany and Mark and was thrilled for their happiness. Yet . . . yet there were times when she saw the way Mark looked into Brittany's eyes and she couldn't help but feel a deep longing in the pit of her stomach. Sometimes Leedy wished she had someone in her life who looked at her the way Mark looked at Brittany. Someone she could confide in. Someone she could tell all of her dreams to. Someone who would hold her in his strong arms, kiss her, and tell her that everything would be all right.

Leedy reassured Brittany that Mr. Hobo's would survive without her and sent her on her way. "Thanks," Brittany said, giving her a goodbye hug.

Just then, Leedy noticed Mark standing at the entrance waiting for his future bride. Brittany gathered up her belongings and waved one last time before she exited. Leedy watched her pinch Mark's rear and smiled. It was impossible for her to be jealous of Brittany for too long. She was just too darn cute to resent.

Leedy contemplated her own love life while she put her purse and jacket in her locker. It had been almost eight months since Brian had broken off their two-year relationship. "We've grown apart," he had told her, and she knew it was true. She cared for Brian and she knew he cared for her, but the last six months they were together it felt as if their romance was based more on habit than on any kind of genuine passion between them. They never seemed to have much to say to one another anymore. Worse still, when he took her in his arms and kissed her she felt . . . she felt . . .

Leedy couldn't describe the way she felt when Brian kissed her. His kisses still tasted sweet, but there was something missing. Something that she ached for, but couldn't define. When Brian kissed her, it felt more like she was kissing an old friend than a lover. The passion that she told herself had once been there was now long gone, and both of them knew it.

It was only after the breakup that she learned that Brian had met another woman. Her name was Angela, and they had been seeing each other for almost a year, an overlap in timing that left Leedy feeling emotionally raw. Oddly, she had never been particularly angry about Brian's unfaithfulness, even if she had not known about it at the time. She now realized that she had sensed the distance between them long before Brian had met Angela. She had recently heard through the grapevine that Brian and Angela were getting married next spring.

Leedy took a deep breath and slammed the locker door shut. There was no point dwelling on ancient history, especially today. She braced herself and headed for the kitchen, suddenly grateful that her evening would be a busy one.

She checked on the kitchen crew, then headed for the dining room to be sure everything was running smoothly there. She replenished the coffee stations, ran the sweeper over some crumb-covered carpeting, and checked to be sure the waiters and waitresses had everything they needed for the dinner rush. After that, she headed back to the kitchen where she prepared several Chocolate Ecstasy Cakes. The recipe was one she had created herself and it had quickly become the most popular dessert item on Mr. Hobo's menu.

Brittany had been right. Judging from the tables filled with college-aged young people and beaming adults, there was surely something going on at the University tonight. In fact, she had never seen Mr. Hobo's so busy. It was well into the dinner hour before she finally found time to schmooze with the customers in the dining room. "How was your meal tonight, sir?" Leedy asked a man in a black turtleneck shirt.

"My soup was cold," he complained.

"Oh, I'm sorry, sir," she said. "May I get you another bowl?"

"No."

"How about a dessert? It's on the house."

"All right," the man in the turtleneck said with a triumphant expression on his face. Leedy motioned for the waiter and one quickly appeared at the table pushing the dessert cart.

"The Chocolate Ecstasy Cake is the house specialty," the waiter said, smiling luminously.

Leedy made her way around the room, charming the clientele as she went. She was in her element, smiling and making jokes with the customers as she made her way through the busy dining room, leaving a trail of happiness behind her.

"And you, young lady?" Leedy asked a pretty, blonde coed in a blue sweater sitting by herself at a table. "How was your dinner?"

"Wonderful," the girl said, with a sweet smile. "I had the shrimp scampi and it was absolutely delicious."

"Thank you," Leedy said. There was something about this lovely girl that made her forget about the hordes of other customers. Something sweet and precious, as if the girl was a single red rose in a thicket of weeds. "I'm so glad you enjoyed your meal," Leedy smiled. "May I offer you a dessert?"

"Maybe . . ." she said. "It's Parents' Night at the University. I'm waiting for my uncle to come back from the restroom."

"Ah," Leedy said. "Parents' Night. That explains the madhouse here this evening."

"There he is now," the young woman said excitedly. "Uncle Terry, would you like a dessert?"

Leedy turned around smiling up at the figure approaching her from behind.

"Hello again," said a low, warm voice that sounded uncomfortably familiar. "Leedy, isn't it?"

"Oh . . . um . . . hi," Leedy stammered, thunderstruck because, there, standing right in front of her, was Terry Foster—the last person in the world she wanted to see. "Nice to see you again, Mr. Foster," she mumbled.

"Call me Terry," he said. Leedy noticed that he was still as gorgeous as he had been earlier that day—a fact that didn't make her feel any better. "I see you've met my niece, Deanna."

"Yes," Leedy said, turning her attention back to the girl. "It is wonderful to meet you."

"It's nice to meet you too," Deanna said, shaking Leedy's hand and smiling from ear to ear. "May I call you Leedy?"

"Of course."

"Deanna took me on a tour of the University," he said. "But it has changed so much since I was a student there a century or so ago . . ."

"Oh, Uncle Terry," Deanna scolded. "You're only thirty."

"And you're eighteen," he said, pretending to choke. "I have socks older than you."

Deanna rolled her eyes and wrinkled her adorable nose.

"Stop teasing," she warned, giving him a playful poke. Leedy sensed a strong affection between them.

Deanna looked at Leedy, as though sizing her up, and then glanced at her uncle. "Please excuse me, Uncle Terry . . . Leedy," she said sweetly. "I need to powder my nose."

Leedy watched her walk off toward the restrooms. She noticed that Deanna had the same tall, lean build and the same confident gait as her uncle.

"Are Deanna's parents here too?" she asked Terry after Deanna turned the corner.

"No," he said, his voice dropping. "Deanna's parents were killed in a car accident about six years ago. Ever since then it's just been the two of us."

"I'm sorry," Leedy said softly, taken aback.

"Thank you," Terry said. "Deanna and I miss them both very much."

"She's a lovely young woman," she added, feeling shaken. "You have obviously done a good job with her. You must be very proud."

"I am," he said. "But I can't take all the credit. Deanna is a great kid. A teenager isn't always as much trouble as people seem to think. She eats her vegetables, doesn't smoke or drink, and makes good grades in school. And she's quite bright."

"Yes. I can tell."

"She's in her first year at the University. She wants to be teacher."

Terry Foster's face beamed when he spoke of Deanna. Indisputably, he had been a good guardian to the girl. Leedy was embarrassed. She remembered tearfully dashing out of his office earlier that day and felt suddenly ashamed of herself.

"Excuse me," said the man in the black turtleneck who was sitting at the table behind them. "Whom do I have to kill to get a cup of hot coffee around here?"

"I'll be happy to get you some coffee, sir," Leedy said. Terry gave the man an annoyed glare. "Have a nice evening, Mr. Foster," she added to Terry, not knowing what else to say. But for some reason, she hesitated to leave his table. She shook his hand and smiled. She didn't want to leave him, but duty called.

By the time she had gone through the dining room with the coffee pot, Terry and Deanna were getting ready to leave. "No dessert?" she asked, trying to hide her disappointment. She had developed an instant fondness for Deanna, and the new-found knowledge that she was an orphan only made her feel even more of an attachment to the girl.

"No thanks, Leedy," Deanna said. "We had better not. My uncle and I are running in a 10k race tomorrow."

"Oh?" she asked. "Is it the one at Baker Park?"

"Yes."

"I'm running in that race, too."

"Are you really?" Deanna gushed, delighted.

"Yes. I usually only run in the 5K races. I'm not a very good distance runner. This is my first 10K race."

"It doesn't matter if you're not a distance runner," Deanna said. "It's all for fun, isn't it? We're in the Cheese City Runners Club. We run in all the 10K races. You should join too."

"I've thought about joining them," Leedy confessed. "But my schedule is so erratic. I just run in the races when I can."

"I hope we see you there," Deanna said happily. "In fact, why don't you meet us there?"

"Well . . . I could . . . I guess . . ."

"It would be fun!" she pressed. "We always warm up by the starting line. You could meet us there right before the race."

Without realizing it, Leedy was nodding. "Okay," she said, not daring to look at Terry Foster. But she could feel him watching her with those brilliant blue eyes of his.

"We'll see you there," he said. Leedy looked up and saw he was looking at her with a lingering look that she couldn't quite read. He smiled at her and then helped Deanna on with her jacket before they headed for the door.

"It was nice to meet you," Deanna called as they left the restaurant. "We'll see you at the race tomorrow."

Chapter Three

Leedy crouched beneath a large maple tree by the starting line and stretched her hamstring muscles. She tried to look nonchalant as she scanned the faces in the crowd. "I'm just looking for Deanna," she told herself. "I don't care if Uncle What's-His-Name shows up or not." But she was nervous. What if she didn't find them? What if she never saw Uncle What's-His-Name again?

Finally, she thought she saw a tall, slender girl in the crowd. Yes, that was Deanna all right. And Terry Foster was standing next to her. They were warming up together on a patch of grass near the starting line. They wore matching black nylon running shorts and yellow t-shirts emblazoned with the words 'CHEESE CITY RUNNER'S CLUB, BAKER PARK 2002 10K RUN" Leedy immediately noticed how Terry looked just as good in his running clothes as he did in the charcoal gray banker's suit. In fact, the sight of his long, muscular legs and well-formed biceps made her heart skip a beat.

She stood up and slowly walked toward them, trying to look disinterested. "Hi, Leedy," Deanna called when she saw her. She looked up, pretending she had not seen them. "Please come join us!"

Terry Foster smiled broadly and waved her over. "Hey there!" he called over the noisy crowd.

"Great day for a run, isn't it?" Deanna gushed when Leedy returned their greeting.

"Yes," she said, coming toward them, trying not to look at Terry.

"Would you like to run with us?" Deanna offered.

"I'm a little rusty," Leedy lied. "I haven't been running as much as I should. I probably would only slow you down."

"We don't mind," Deanna assured her. "Uncle Terry usually beats me anyway. And we're not here to compete. We're here for the fun of it. We won't care if you fall behind."

"All right," Leedy said, stealing a shy glance toward Terry. "But, like I said before. I'm not a long-distance runner. Don't let me slow you down."

"We can all start together, anyway," Terry offered.

"All right," she said with an indifferent shrug.

"You won't mind if I take off like a bullet, would you?" he asked her, leaning in closer. "I've been running quite a bit lately. I'm training to run in a marathon this spring. I'm in great shape for a 10K run."

"Is that so?" she asked, taking in the smug, amused expression on his handsome face.

"Oh, yes," he said. "Deanna will tell you."

Deanna nodded and rolled her eyes. "It's true," she said. "He's been running every day."

"I'm up to fifteen miles a day," he gloated. "As a matter of fact, I might just win this race."

"Win it?" Leedy asked, skeptically.

"Yes," he said. "I have a good feeling I'm going to win today."

"Good luck," Leedy said, uncertain of what to make of his sudden smugness.

Deanna rolled her eyes again and laughed. "Don't mind him, Leedy. He's just teasing you. And stop bragging, Uncle Terry."

"You're right," he said with a wink. "But I'm still going to win the race."

"He probably will win," Deanna said to Leedy, with a shrug. "But still . . ."

Just then a red-faced man with a megaphone announced the start of the race. All of the runners gave their bodies one last stretch and then headed for the starting line. Leedy, Terry, and Deanna made their way through the crowd until they found a place near the front. Leedy stood in between Terry and Deanna. She glanced over at Terry and saw that he was watching her with a big, happy grin on his face.

"Good luck," he said.

"On your mark!" shouted the red-faced man into the megaphone.

"You too," Leedy said. "But I only run for the exercise. This is all in fun, you know."

"Get set!" yelled the man.

"Well then," Terry said, with a confident smirk. "Have fun."

"GO!" screamed the man into the megaphone. A whistle blew and Leedy took off, running at top speed. She knew she had little hope of winning, but if she could gain some distance early in the race, she might have a chance at doing well. "Coming through," she said, as she sprinted past Terry. He only smiled and waved her on as he kept running, not missing a single beat in his steady, smooth stride.

She dashed as fast as her legs could carry her ahead of him. Something about Terry's cocky confidence made her determined to do well. Within a minute she had overtaken Deanna and then another runner. Despite what she had told Deanna, Leedy had been running quite a bit lately. It was a coping strategy for the ongoing stress of her busy life. Even so, she was surprised at how easily she passed the other racers, who seemed to be moving slower than they should.

The sun was shining, but it was not hot and the crowds of spectators that lined the street were cheering her on. So she ran. She ran as hard and as strong as she had ever run before. She glanced over her shoulder and saw that Terry was behind her, his long, taut legs moving in a perfect, uniform stride, gaining on her with every stroke. She pumped her legs harder, trying to put some pavement between herself and the other runners.

Leedy's legs cooperated, at first. But soon, her breathing was becoming more ragged. She ignored it and ran ahead, pushing her legs to move still faster, if that was even possible. A small twinge of pain developed in her left knee but by blowing short puffs of air out of her mouth, she was able to keep going.

From time to time, she would grab a paper cup of water from one of the spectators and gulp it down. But she realized that every time she did, it slowed her down. Soon a nagging ache developed in her knee, which started to radiate to her shin. She had also developed a persistent stabbing pain in her right side. She leaned into the stitch a bit and kept on running.

Leedy knew her strength as a runner didn't lie in her ability to run long distances, but in her ability to sprint shorter distances quickly. A 10K race was not her strong suit, and now she could feel her strength ebbing away. But she wanted to do well in the race, if only to prove to herself she was capable of it.

She looked ahead of her, trying not to think about the other runners slowly gaining ground behind her, when it suddenly dawned on her that all the runners who had been ahead of her were now nowhere to be seen. She was surprised and happy when she realized she had somehow managed to take the lead. This was certainly a new experience for her and she relished her victory. But her triumph was short-lived, because a quick glance behind her told her that Terry Foster was steadily catching up.

Leedy gritted her teeth and implored her legs to keep moving. She could see the finish line less than a block away, and she could hear the shouts of the spectators, but she knew her exhausted body was faltering. Her lungs felt as if they were going to burst, her knee was screaming in pain, and the small stitch in her side had become excruciating.

"Coming through," said a cheerful voice from behind her. Leedy felt a rush of wind as Terry ran past. She tried to catch up with him and for a few harrowing seconds, she thought she might be able to maintain her lead, but the ache that coursed through her body was too strong. He strode past her with a smooth ease and crossed the finish line only seconds before her.

"Arrgghh!" Leedy groaned as she crossed the line and collapsed on a grassy incline. Deanna soon followed behind her, laughing and hooting in youthful glee.

"Wow!" she shouted, jumping up and down. "That was great! Uncle Terry came in first and you came in second! Women never beat men in these races! I thought you didn't run fast!"

But Leedy was beyond conversation. She lay in the grass panting as she waited for her knee to stop throbbing and her heart to cease pounding and for the burning pain in her chest to go away. Every breath was anguish. Plus, she was certain she'd never be able to walk again.

Leedy knew she had committed the ultimate runner's sin and she was annoyed with herself. She had broken her stride, almost from the starting line.

"Need some help?" a voice from above called to her. She squinted into the bright morning sunshine and saw Terry leaning over her, holding out his hand. She grabbed it and he hoisted her up.

"You need to work on your finish line technique," he said, handing her a paper cup of water. "Here, drink this. You look as if you could use it."

"Thanks," Leedy gasped as she took the water and gulped it down.

"Great race," he said, his blue eyes dancing. Deanna followed behind him, jumping up and down with excitement. Leedy noted that neither Terry not Deanna looked any the worse for wear. In fact, they had barely broken a sweat. "I think I may have overdone it," she said, pushing back her wet, sticky hair. He handed her another paper cup of water and watched her drain it.

"You'll be all right in a couple of minutes," he said,

letting his hand slip softly onto the small of her back. Despite the fact that every muscle in her body was still screaming in pain, the feel of Terry's strong hand touching her sent ripples of pleasure coursing through her body, along with needles of electricity all the way down to her toes.

"Great race," Leedy repeated.

"You, too," Terry said. "You're quite an athlete." He stood there, momentarily, looking into her eyes and smiling.

"Let's go, Uncle Terry," Deanna said. "You promised we would go to brunch after the race. I'm starving!"

"Great idea," he said. "Perhaps Leedy would like to join us?"

"Yes!" Deanna exclaimed. "Please come with us, Leedy! We're going to go home first to grab showers, but we can meet you there. We are going to the Northern Inn. They have a wonderful buffet on the weekends."

"It will be fun," Terry coaxed. "Or, at least, more fun than hyperventilating. Come on, Leedy. Come with us."

It was a tempting offer, but the pain in her knee screamed in protest and she knew it was going to be another busy day at Mr. Hobo's. "Thanks for the invitation," she said. "But I can't. I have to work this afternoon."

"Oh . . . darn," Deanna said with feeling.

"Maybe next time," Terry offered, still maddeningly handsome.

"Yes, maybe. And thanks again," Leedy said. "But duty calls." She handed Terry back the paper cup before she limped away, trying vainly to exit with as much dignity as she could muster.

Chapter Four

Leedy spent an hour soaking in the bathtub, hoping the hot water would soothe not only her aching body, but her aching pride as well. Every muscle felt as though it had been worked over by a prize fighter. Her knee was still tender to the touch and the condition of her throbbing back remained precarious. But her sore muscles were not the only thing that was giving her remorse.

She was pleased she had placed so well in the race, but . . . Leedy had come to the difficult realization that her actions over the past few days had been embarrassing, and she was mortified. Her hasty exit from Terry Foster's office and her overly competitive behavior at the race were childish, to say the least.

She sank deeper into the hot water, trying to forget the past two days. She was usually such a levelheaded person—but ever since her first meeting with Terry Foster, she had been acting like a blockhead. She was tongue-tied and awkward whenever he was anywhere near. What on earth had gotten into her?

The only conclusion she could come to was that, for reasons that couldn't be explained, the loan officer ignited a side of her that no one else had ever seen. A side that was electrifying, but not altogether rational.

Leedy lay in the tub and let her mind wander. She thought about the way Terry's strong, muscular legs moved when he ran and the way his hand had felt against her back. She closed her eyes, and let the warmth of the bath envelope her. "Okay," she told herself out loud. "So, he's handsome. So what? Brian was handsome too, remember? So he makes your heart go pitty-pat. You're a big girl. You can handle this. But don't forget, he's a bit arrogant. And . . ." She couldn't think of anything else, so the sentence remained unfinished.

She searched for a theory that would somehow define why she had allowed this man to so quickly and effectively upset her apple cart. A theory that would explain the unsettling effect he had on her life. Terry was a mystery to be pondered, a problem to be solved, and she was determined to put him in his proper place, at least mentally. "So what if he's handsome?" she asked again. "He's trouble . . . and I should stay as far away from him as I can." She made the statement out loud with as much feeling as she could gather, but it still somehow lacked conviction.

Leedy sighed and stepped out of the tub, reaching for a towel. The soft, fluffy terry cloth felt good as she patted herself dry. She lingered on the special places of her flawless body. Places where the nubby fabric felt delicious rubbing against her skin. She closed her eyes again and wondered what it would feel like to be held in Terry's strong arms.

"Stop it!" she said out loud. She was annoyed with the way she had so quickly forgotten her decision to steer clear of this man. This man who had turned down her application for the small business loan she needed to open her restaurant.

Leedy finished drying off and set about with the task of putting herself together enough to go to work. It was her weekend to work the "turn around" shift, which meant the dinner rush on Friday night and then the day shift on Saturday. It made for a long, grueling experience, especially since Parents' Night really meant Parents' Weekend. But she didn't mind working. The long hours would keep her mind off her recent disappointments . . . and off Terry Foster.

She dressed in the black tuxedo (which luckily was holding up well, considering there were no all-night, one-hour dry cleaners) and a fresh, starched white blouse. She applied her make-up and blew dry her long, straight hair until it was soft and glossy again. She pulled it back into a ponytail and fastened it with a beautiful silver hairclip she had bought at an antique store. She looked in the mirror and felt hesitantly pleased by what she saw. Her skin was peaches and cream and her chestnut brown eyes were bright and clear. She looked decidedly good, all things considered.

By the time she arrived at Mr. Hobo's an hour later, Leedy was feeling like her old self again. Well, almost. Her first stop was in the kitchen, which had fallen woefully behind in setting up for the soon-to-arrive lunch crowd. She spent an hour chopping vegetables for the salads. Then she prepared more Chocolate Ecstasy cakes, which had been selling like the proverbial hotcakes since Friday.

It was well into the afternoon before she was finally able to head into the dining room. She ran the sweeper around the tables, poured coffee for customers, and took care of one hundred little disasters that came up along the way. Leedy liked it when Mr. Hobo's was busy. It was then that she was in her true domain. Crowds of hungry diners and a chaotic kitchen didn't ruffle her feathers. In fact she loved it when the heat was on and she ran Mr. Hobo's as if she had been doing it for ten years instead of six months.

She was restocking the supplies at the coffee station, her head buried deep inside the cabinet, when she heard a voice from above. "Excuse me. I'm looking for Leedy Collins." She jumped, startled, and banged her head painfully on the inside of the cabinet. She looked up, rubbing the bump that had quickly popped up, to see Terry Foster standing over her.

"Oh," she gasped. "Mr. Foster. I didn't hear you."

"I'm sorry if I snuck up behind you," he said, helping her to her feet.

"It's okay," she said, trying to compose herself.

"Did you hurt your head?"

"No," she said, her ears ringing. "I'm fine."

"Have you recovered from the race?"

"Yes. And you?"

"Yes," he said with an amused, easy smile. He was dressed in pressed khakis and a soft denim shirt. He looked as though he had just stepped out of a page from a magazine. "I'm all done gloating, thank you. I'm here because we never finished our meeting yesterday. I had some free time this afternoon. I was hoping you would have a few minutes to discuss your loan application."

"Oh?" Leedy said, her ears perking up at the mention of the word *loan.*

"Have you had lunch?" he asked.

"No. Not yet."

He was standing close enough for her to smell the clean aroma of his soap and aftershave. It was a wonderful aroma. "You shouldn't skip lunch," he said. "Especially after running the race you ran this morning."

"Thanks for the tip."

"Can you take a break?" he asked. There was a sensuous quality to his voice that made all of Leedy's resolutions from that morning a faraway memory.

"I can't leave the restaurant," she said. "But . . . um . . . we can eat lunch here . . . if you don't mind, that is."

"This is a restaurant, isn't it?" he noted. "A very nice restaurant."

"Yes, it is," she said. "Give me a few minutes to check on things and I'll meet you in the back dining room. It's quieter there."

"I'll see you in a few minutes."

She went to the kitchen and spoke with the chef. The lunch rush was over and dinner was still hours away, and everything seemed to be running smoothly, for now. She was headed back to the dining room when she spotted Brittany coming into the kitchen.

"Can you cover for me for about a half-hour?" Leedy asked. She didn't want any interruptions during her meeting with Terry.

"Sure," Brittany replied. "Are you going out?"

"No," she explained. "The man from the bank is here and we are going to have a meeting. He's here to talk about my loan application."

Brittany looked through the portal of the big, swinging stainless steel doors that led to the dining room. "Since when does the bank make house calls?" she asked, scanning the restaurant. "Is that him? The guy in the blue jean shirt and the khaki's?"

"Yes."

"Hey, he's kind of cute," Brittany said, standing on her tiptoes to get a better view. "No, wait . . . I take that back. He's not kind of cute, Leedy. This guy is totally hot! Where did you get him?"

"It's not what you think, Brit," she explained, feeling her face flush. "Mr. Foster is here to talk about the bank loan."

"I thought they declined it," Brittany said.

"They did, but the loan officer is here to give me some advice."

"Uh huh."

"He is!"

"I believe you," Brittany said, but the grin on her face told Leedy otherwise.

"Please, Brit," she said. "This is important to me."

Brittany knew better than anyone how much Leedy wanted her dream of opening her own restaurant to come true. She looked at Leedy and realized she was all but jumping out of her skin. "Okay, okay," Brittany said. "I'll cover for you. Now, breathe, girl, breathe!"

Leedy took a deep breath and let it out slowly. "Good idea," she said.

"Is this good news?" Brittany asked. "Is the bank going to reconsider your application?"

"I hope so," Leedy said as she turned toward the door. "Or he's here to tell me to go jump in a lake. Oh . . . would you mind bringing us some clam chowder? And something cold to drink? And anything else that looks good?"

"For a meeting with this guy," Brittany purred. "I would go for white wine and oysters if I were you," She couldn't resist teasing her one last time. Brittany gave her friend a seductive wink and headed back to the kitchen.

Leedy turned to walk into the dining room but caught herself. She examined her reflection in the stainless steel doors and ran a hand through her hair, smoothing a tress of long, shiny brown hair that had escaped from the silver hairclip. She freshened her lipstick from the tube of Brandied Ginger she kept in the pocket of her jacket. She smacked her lips together, took one more deep breath, and pushed through the swinging doors.

Terry Foster was sitting at a table in the farthest corner of the restaurant. He was flipping through some papers from inside a battered briefcase that sat on the table in front of him. "Thanks for waiting," she said, feeling suddenly nervous. Could this man really give her a second chance for her restaurant?

He stood up and pulled the chair out for her. She took a seat and he sat down across from her. He smiled broadly and pulled still more papers from the briefcase. "I was in the area," he said. "You were so upset when you left my office yesterday. I thought I would stop by so we could talk about your loan application . . . calmly."

"I apologize for the way I behaved," Leedy said. "Believe it or not, I don't normally pout when I don't get my way. It's just that I was so disappointed. I've worked hard to get to this place, Mr. Foster, and I desperately want my loan to be approved. I know that's no excuse, but . . ."

"Call me Terry," he said. "And I understand how you

feel. Besides, you were mild compared to some of my other clients. But that's why I'm here, Leedy. I think if we put our heads together, we can figure out a way for you to make your restaurant become a reality."

"So the bank is willing to reexamine my application?" she asked.

"I didn't say that," he said. "In fact, to be perfectly honest, you're not ready yet."

"I could be ready."

"Not yet," he said. "You still have some more work to do."

"I could be ready today if your bank would approve my loan."

"It isn't that easy."

"Why not?" she asked. She almost added 'Terry,' but she caught herself. Leedy had already started to think of him as 'Terry,' not 'Mr. Foster,' but she didn't want to say it. It still seemed too personal.

Just then, Brittany appeared at the table carrying a heavy tray laden with food. "Hi," she said, smiling her angelic grin.

"Hi," Terry said, returning the smile with a brilliant one of his own. Brittany placed two piping hot bowls of clam chowder onto the table and began to unload glasses of iced tea.

"How are you two doing today?" she asked.

"Why, just fine. Thank you," he said.

Brittany glanced at Leedy and gave her another diabolical grin. "Isn't Leedy pretty?" she asked Terry, wrinkling her precious pug nose.

"Yes, she is," he said with an equally devilish smile. Brittany set down a large bowl of caesar salad and gave a speechless Leedy another wicked wink before disappearing back into the kitchen.

"Don't mind her," Leedy stammered, making a mental note to pinch Brittany later. "Brittany is getting married next month and the stress of making the wedding plans has left her quite insane. We're hoping it is only temporary."

"I don't mind," Terry said. "She's adorable. Besides, she's only pointing out the obvious. You are attractive." Leedy didn't mention that Brittany had said the same thing about him.

Terry was looking at her, a soft smile playing on his lips. She returned the gaze and was instantly lost in his blue eyes. He leaned closer to her, staring into her face for a lingering moment and she thought . . . hoped . . . that he might lean across the small table and kiss her.

"Um . . ." he said suddenly, clearing his throat. "I'm sorry . . . where was I?"

"We were discussing my loan application," Leedy said, feeling warm all over.

"Yes," he said. "Your loan application . . . Um . . . I see that you have some funds already set aside in your savings account."

"I try to put away as much as I can every week. It isn't close to what I need, but . . ."

"It's growing into a tidy sum of money," he noted. "But, you're right, it's just a drop in the bucket. However, it shows that you know how to manage your money and that you're serious about your business."

"Thank you," she said. "I *am* serious about the business of opening a restaurant."

"Clearly," he said. His eyes lingered on her again, and

she again almost fell into the dreaminess of his eyes, but this time she caught herself.

"What does the bank want me to do?" she asked. She hated to wheedle, especially to Terry, but a flicker of hope was sitting across the table from her and she wasn't about to let it pass her by.

"Have you ever taken any classes in accounting?" Terry asked.

"No," she said. "At least not since my junior year of high school."

"Business Management?"

"I'm sure I took a few business classes in college."

"Human Resources?"

"No. But I've been the manager of Mr. Hobo's for the past six months." She ate a spoonful of soup. "I deal with human resources issues every day. I hire people. And fire them when I have to . . ."

"But six months isn't a very long time," he said and he too took a spoonful of soup.

"It is in the food industry," Leedy said. "I work fourteen hours a day, Mr. Foster."

"Call me Terry," he reminded her. "This soup is fantastic, by the way. And I'm sure you're a hard worker, Leedy. But there's more to running a restaurant than a willingness to put in long hours."

"I know," she said.

"A restaurant proprietor needs to be an expert not just on the day-to-day operations of providing food to the customers, but also in accounting matters, human resources, food preparation . . ."

"I'm a chef, remember?" she reminded him. "As a matter of fact, I made this salad."

"It's delicious," Terry said. "But surely you realize that no one person can do *everything*. You need to have a plan, Leedy. A well-thought-out strategy that will prove to the bank that your restaurant will be successful."

She said nothing. He was making sense, of course, but nonetheless, Leedy didn't like what he was saying. "Go on," she said.

"I will," Terry said. "First of all, have you thought about the location of your restaurant?"

"Yes, of course."

"You allocated a reasonable amount of money in your budget for the lease, but you were vague about where your restaurant was going to be. That's an important consideration for the bank, don't you think?"

"Yes," Leedy said. "But I need approval from the bank before I can negotiate a lease. No one will talk to me about a lease until I have a firm financial commitment."

"I understand your problem," Terry said. "But the bank needs specific information to determine if your restaurant is a sound venture. Have you thought about buying a place instead of renting? Property values are going up in Madison. It may be a good time to invest in real estate instead of signing a lease. And you wouldn't have to worry about a landlord kicking you out when your contract is up."

"How could I possibly afford to buy a building?" she asked.

"These are the sort of things that the bank considers before it approves a loan," he said.

"I can see your point of view, Mr. Foster, but . . ."

"And you didn't allow for nearly enough funds to get you through those first critical months after you open."

"I thought it was sufficient," she said.

"You wouldn't last a month with the small amount of money you requested," he told her.

Leedy set down her fork and cocked her head to one side. "But your bank denied my application, remember?" she said. "What chance would I have of getting a loan approved for even more money?"

"Your application was not denied because you were asking for too much money," he said. "Your application was denied because the bank didn't think your proposal was a safe investment. And we're a bank, not a fairy godmother."

She winced. She knew she was wearing her heart on her sleeve and she did not want to. "This is all good advice," she said. "But the restaurant business is not the same as . . . say, opening up an antique shop or a gas station. There are health code standards and payroll issues that are unique to food preparation, not to mention the high degree of competition between restaurants and the fickleness of the customers. I've worked in this business for a long time, Mr. Foster, and, believe me, there are a million variables to think of. I've tried to take everything into account and I think I've done a fairly good job of it."

"You have," he said. "But my field of expertise is strictly on the business and finance side of things. That's something that every business needs to consider. And I think I can help you put things in focus."

"Okay," she said. "What do you think I need to do to get my restaurant off the ground?"

"It's funny you should ask," Terry said and held up a yellow pad of paper. She could see that several pages were already filled with small, neat handwriting. "After you left yesterday, I took a second look at your loan application and jotted down a few notes."

Leedy scanned the first page. "I can't do all these things!" she said. "It would take forever."

"You can too do all those things," Terry said. "You can and you will. Because you, Leedy Collins, are the kind of woman who will make her restaurant dream come true. Whatever the costs. It may take years for it to happen, but . . ."

"Years?" Her heart sank.

"Years—and the sooner you get started the sooner you will be ready."

Leedy definitely didn't like what he was saying, but she had to admit the items listed on the yellow pad made sense. She nodded and watched him from across the small table. He smiled and, once again, she wished he would lean over the table and kiss her. An inappropriate gesture perhaps, but she wished for it all the same.

"Okay," she said, finally. "I guess it wouldn't hurt to consider your notes. I'm not promising I'll follow through with all of your suggestions. But I'll consider them."

"Good enough," he said and sipped his iced tea.

She flipped through the pages of the legal pad as they silently ate their lunch. Terry watched her with a look in his eye that she couldn't quite identify. Was it admiration? Sympathy? Desire?

Finally he looked at his watch. "Oh, boy," he exclaimed, suddenly jumping up from his chair. "I lost track of the time! I'm in big trouble."

"What's wrong?" Leedy asked.

"I'm late. I promised Deanna I would take her shopping for shoes." By the pained expression on his face, she knew Terry was not thrilled with the idea.

"That sounds like fun," Leedy offered.

"For you maybe," he groaned. "I'm not much of a shopper. Oddly, it seems to be Deanna's favorite pastime. And since I have all the credit cards, she's most insistent that I tag along. Besides, you can never have enough shoes, can you?"

"No," Leedy said, smiling. Deanna was certainly a girl after her own heart. "You really can't have enough shoes."

He stood up, apologizing for leaving so abruptly. She assured him it was quite all right. She was surprised how her feelings for Terry had gone from worry to warmth in a matter of moments. She stood up and shook his hand. "Thank you for stopping by, Mr. Foster," she said formally.

"Thank you," he said. He looked her in the eyes and suddenly took her by both of her shoulders and gently shook her. "And, for the last time, my name is Terry!"

"Terry," she said, grinning.

"See you around," he said.

He made it as far as the coffee station before he turned back and walked toward her. "By the way," he said. "A night class called Small Business Management starts next week at the University. You may want to consider signing up."

Leedy shrugged. "I guess it couldn't hurt."

"Good," he said, turning to go. "I'll see you there. I'm the class instructor."

Chapter Five

The classroom was crowded and noisy when Leedy arrived. The room was buzzing with lively conversation from far more students than she had expected would be there. She found an empty desk in the third row, close enough to keep an eye on the attractive instructor, but not too close as to appear overly enthusiastic. She spotted Terry as soon as he arrived in the classroom. He had been blessed with a charisma that allowed him to walk into any room at any time and have everyone's eyes turn to him. He had a way of making his presence known with minimal effort, even in a crowded and noisy classroom. He set his briefcase down on the desk in the front of the room and looked at his watch.

The sight of him took her breath away.

Terry spoke amicably to the pupils hovering about his desk. His blue eyes were alive with enthusiasm, his brown curly hair was tousled in a boyish disarray and he was, at least from Leedy's point-of-view, incredibly handsome.

"Rats," she thought to herself. "Why does he have to be so gosh darn good-looking?"

As if he could read her mind, Terry looked up and glanced in her direction. He moved his eyebrows up and down in a greeting and beamed. He was pleased to see her.

"All right everyone," Terry said, standing up and facing the students. "We've a lot of material to cover tonight, so let's get started." The classroom quieted to a murmur of shuffling papers and shifting chairs as everyone settled down and took their seat. "My name is Terry Foster," he continued, flashing his gorgeous smile. "And I'll be your instructor for the next six weeks."

He wore a pair of faded blue jeans and a blue button-down oxford shirt. Leedy liked how he looked in his casual clothes. Like a college boy, only sexier. She scanned the room. There seemed to be an unusually high ratio of young women in the classroom, most of whom were watching Terry with ardent interest. One woman in particular caught Leedy's eye. She was sitting in the front row, directly in front of Terry's desk. She was attractive, with perfectly coifed blond hair and dark sultry eyes. She wore an expensive brown suede skirt and a plum-colored silk blouse. Leedy wished she had worn something more flattering than the faded blue jeans and navy blue turtleneck she had chosen. Suddenly she felt out of place, as if she had shown up to a ladies' tea party wearing army boots. She watched as the blond woman shook her long shiny hair and fluttered her eyelashes at Terry, all the while smiling at him seductively.

"As I'm sure you all know, this is a class in Small Business Management," he said, returning the blond woman's smile with one of his own. "I've spoken with many of you and I know you're here for different reasons. By way of introduction, I would like to go around the room and have each student introduce him or herself, and tell everyone why you're taking the class." Terry nodded to the woman sitting on the farthest corner of the first row. "Betty?"

"I'm Betty Fulbright," said a soft-spoken woman. "I'm hoping to start up a custom-made quilting business on the internet."

"Joyce Clay," said the woman seated next to her. "And I'm just here to expand my professional horizons."

"A noble ambition," Terry noted. "Next?"

"I'm Krissy Montgomery," cooed the blond woman in front of him. "I'm a financial planner in town and I run my own office. I'm here to learn more about my customers' small business needs so that I can better serve them." Leedy fought the urge to roll her eyes. Krissy Montgomery's voice and manner, like the rest of her, was perfect. Even her name was adorable.

"I'm Brad Mercer," said the man seated at the desk next to Krissy. "I want to get a better handle on my home-improvement business."

"Charlotte Renner, and I'm opening a day care center."

"Mike Lawrence. I have a small accounting firm in town and I'm here to better serve my customers. Just like Miss Montgomery." The man gave Krissy a meaningful look, which she ignored. It seemed she only had eyes for the instructor.

The students took turns, one by one, introducing themselves and telling why they were taking the class. Leedy was slowly coming to the realization that she was not the only one in the room with a lifelong dream.

"Leedy Collins," she said shyly when it was her turn.

"And I want to open a restaurant someday." Krissy Montgomery looked over her shoulder at Leedy through wary eyes. Her mouth turned down tightly for just a brief second; then she looked away.

The woman sitting next to Leedy looked up suddenly and smiled at her. "I guess it's my turn," she said. "My name is Jo Anne Phillips, and I want to open a restaurant someday too."

Leedy and Jo Anne Phillips examined each other for a long moment. "We'll have to talk," Jo Anne whispered. Leedy nodded in agreement.

The rest of the class sped by. Leedy quickly forgot to worry about the blond in the front row because she was too busy taking notes. Terry led a lively discussion about the planning and implementing of a new business which raised points she had never considered. She wrote down every word with many asterisks and parentheses, noting the many things she wanted to further research later.

It ended all too soon. Before she knew it, the class was over and it was time to go. Leedy was still fervently writing in her notebook when she heard a voice behind her. "Ahem," the voice said, and she looked up to see Terry standing in front of her desk.

"Oh," she said, startled. She had been so lost in her writing she had not noticed that the class was almost empty. Even Jo Anne was gone. "I'm sorry I'm taking so long," she said. "I just wanted to write down an idea I had for the restaurant while it was still fresh in my mind."

"That's okay," he said. "I'm glad to see you found the class so inspirational. May I walk you to your car?"

Her heart skipped a beat at the prospect of Terry walking her anywhere. "Okay," she said. She looked around the room. The other students had all shuffled out of the room and some were lingering in the hallway. For a fleeting second, Leedy thought she spotted the blond-haired woman from the front row—Krissy somebody—lingering just outside the door to the classroom. But by the time Terry had helped her collect her books, the shadow was gone. She pulled on the pumpkin orange sweater her mother had knit for her and they headed out the door.

The night was cool as they walked toward the parking lot. The temperature had dropped, letting everyone know that winter was on the way. Leedy shivered from the sudden chill, yet she delighted in the cool dark sky. The autumn air felt good against her face as she and Terry fell into a relaxed, comfortable pace. It felt so right, so good, to be walking next to him. It felt as comfortable as the soft wool of her sweater and as effortless as the beating of her heart. She could almost imagine slipping her hand inside of his as they walked along.

"So?" Terry asked. "Aren't you going to tell me?"

"Tell you what?"

"Tell me about the idea you have for your restaurant?"

"The idea?"

"Yes," Terry said. "You said you were writing down an idea for your restaurant . . ."

"Oh!" She blushed. Something about being around this incredibly handsome man turned her brain into mashed bananas. "Oh . . . um . . . I was thinking about the open house I'd have after my restaurant finally gets started. A grand opening extravaganza."

"Sounds interesting," he said. "Tell me all about it."

"I would serve a buffet. A very elaborate buffet. With

every dish on the menu and maybe a few that aren't. It would be a buffet like you've never seen before."

"Yummy," he said. "It sounds delicious. But I don't remember you allocating for an open house in your start-up costs. How do you plan to pay for this, Miss Money Bags Collins?"

"Oh, no!" she groaned. "You sure know how to take the wind out of a girl's sails, Mr. Black Ink Foster. We're not going to talk about money again, are we?"

"Yes," he said, taking his fleece jacket off and slipping it over her shoulders. "You better take this. It's getting chilly out here."

"Thank you," she said, feeling the warmth of the fabric. "Well . . . of course I would charge admittance to the open house," she said. "But the idea of having a grand opening is to get as many people in the door as possible. The more people I can get to come into my restaurant, the better the chances they'll be back, right?"

"Right. Will you serve wine?"

"Yes, but I won't go crazy. Just a few special vintages I know of . . . priced appropriately, of course."

"Of course. How about desserts?"

"So many desserts it would make your mouth water."

"And you'll take all of that into account when you set the price for the open house buffet, correct?" Terry asked.

"Correct," she nodded. "It will have to be a good price or people won't come. Maybe I could charge a discounted admittance price and include most of the open house costs with my loan application figures. Do you think the bank would approve something like that?"

"The bank might raise an eyebrow," he said. "But they'd understand that establishing a client base is important to your new business. They'd probably go for it." Terry stopped, putting a hand on each of her shoulders. "Now you're thinking like a business woman, Leedy," he said, squeezing her arms gently. It was the second time he had taken her by the shoulders that way. And she liked it.

"Well, I'm glad you finally recognize my business savvy," she said, beaming with pride.

"Don't worry," Terry said, falling back into step beside her. "I've noticed your business savvy, along with all your other fine qualities." They walked on through the quiet night. "You should also talk with Jo Anne Phillips," he added.

"I plan on it. Do you know her?"

"Yes. I met Jo Anne when her husband came to the bank asking for help in starting up his dental practice. She has been a soccer mom for a few years, but before that she had fifteen years of experience as a restaurant manager. Maybe you and Jo Anne can . . . What's the matter?"

She couldn't help it. Something about Terry's expression as he talked made her burst into peals of uncontrollable giggles.

"What's so funny?" he asked, defensively.

"Nothing," Leedy said, trying to stop laughing. "I'm sorry . . . I don't mean to be rude."

"Well, you find something hysterically funny," he said. "Come on, now. Spit it out. What is it?"

"Okay," she said. "But you asked for it . . . I thought, for a moment, that you were flirting with me, Mr. Foster. But now I realize it was only my imagination."

"But I was flirting."

"Ha!" she said, between peals of laughter. "You were too busy talking about business stuff, Terry. As usual. You can't flirt, because you have a one-track mind that can think of one and only one subject."

"A one-track mind? Me?"

"Yes, you," she said triumphantly.

"What are you talking about?" Terry asked, an expression of both exasperation and delight on his face. They had stopped walking and were standing on the outer edges of the campus parking lot.

"I suddenly realized that ever since the moment I first met you, you have talked about one thing and one thing only. Hence, my theory that you have a one-track mind."

"You misunderstand. I have been a perfect gentleman," Terry said, inching closer to her. "And it hasn't been easy on me."

"All the same," Leedy said, enjoying the warm feeling of his body so close to hers. "You do have a one-track mind. Unfortunately, that track is for business matters only."

"Business?"

"Yes, business."

"Is that so?" he said, looking wounded.

"Yes!" She knew they were both flirting shamelessly, but neither one of them seemed to care.

"Business matters only?"

"That's what I said."

"That's a dirty lie," Terry said, moving closer toward her. His face was inches from hers. So close she could almost feel the end-of-the-day stubble on his cheek. He slid his arm around her waist and pulled her gently to him.

"It isn't a lie," she said breathlessly as she squirmed away from him.

"Is too," he said. He was as close as he could be now,

his face about to touch hers when, suddenly, a loud blast of a car horn sounded, making them both jump. The car horn blared again, and she looked up and saw a car in the far parking lot. An arm went out the window and waved, then the car pulled away.

"Who was that?" Leedy asked.

"Probably someone from the class," Terry said, frowning.

"It is getting late," she said. "There's my car right over there . . ."

Terry led her to the Jeep. She pulled out her car keys and turned to him to say goodbye. "I'll see you in class on Thursday," she said and handed him his jacket. "Oh, and, by the way, you do too have a one-track mind."

Terry stopped her from putting the key into the lock by pulling her close to him. He held her tightly for a moment, his breath warm against her cheek. "I do not," he whispered, soft and husky, into her ear. "And I could prove otherwise, Ms. Collins, if you have some free time."

"Why, Mr. Foster," she said, with all the indignation of a compromised southern belle. "You may just have more on your mind after all." She opened up her car door and climbed in behind the wheel. "It is a pity that I'm your student," she said and firmly shut the car door. She rolled down the window and beamed at him. "I'm a big fan of protocol." She waved out the window and started the engine of the car.

"Yeah, but it is only a six-week class!" he called to her as she drove away.

Chapter Six

"Six weeks, twice a week—every Tuesday and Thursday," Leedy explained. "I can't believe I've already been to three classes! The time is flying by!"

"Are you sure it's enough time?" Brittany asked.

"Enough time for what?" Leedy asked, not understanding why her friend had a mischievous grin on her face.

"Enough time to charm your professor into falling for you," she teased. "I know it won't take you long. But still, these things are not always instantaneous."

"What are you talking about?" Leedy asked.

"As if you don't know."

"I don't know."

"Admit it, Leedy."

"Admit what?"

"Admit you have a crush on the hunky banker."

Leedy only rolled her eyes.

"Liar, liar, pants on fire," Brittany taunted. "Come on! This is me you're talking to, remember? Don't forget, I'm the one getting married in one month. I understand exactly what you're going through."

"Oh? Do you?"

"Yes, I do. In fact, I understand it better than you do."

Leedy raised her eyebrows. "Oh," she said, her voice suspicious. "Then tell me, She Who Knows All, what exactly am I going through?"

"You're in the 'Mr. Wonderful Is Not Supposed To Appear Until Step 28 Of My Master Plan. Therefore, I Am Not Really Falling For This Perfect Guy' phase," Brittany retorted with a smug expression on her face. "Except that you're falling for him, Leedy. Next comes the attraction/attraction phase."

There was a ring of truth to what her friend said, but Leedy didn't want to admit it. "What's that phase all about?"

"That's when you both stop tiptoeing around each other and decide you're indeed really and truly falling for one another. That's when you both stop pretending and start to really enjoy being with each other. This is a great phase to be in! So admit it!"

"Okay," Leedy said, feeling her cheeks turn pink. "I admit it! I'm a little bit attracted to him. Does it show that much?"

"Only to the trained eye," Brittany said. "I had the same dopey expression on my face after I met Mark."

"What dopey expression?"

"That look in your eye! It's like . . . like you're on Cloud Terry."

Leedy blushed, embarrassed that she was so transparent.

"It's okay to feel that way. In fact, it is wonderful to feel that way! So you see, Leedy, I know exactly what you're going through after all."

"I'm not as far gone as you were over Mark."

"Yes you are."

"What makes you say that?" Leedy asked.

"I can just tell," Brittany said. "Because I remember how I was. I was excited and happy, but at the same time, anxious. I couldn't wait to see him again, but I didn't want to be appear to be overly interested either. I had trouble concentrating at work and I sometimes forgot to eat. I found Mark creeping into my thoughts all the time, especially at night when I was lying in bed."

Leedy was speechless. Brittany did know exactly what she was going through.

"At least, that's the way it was for me," Brittany added. "At first, I tried to run away from my feelings for Mark— just like you are trying to run away from your feelings for Terry. I pretended I didn't really care about him, except I couldn't get him out of my head. Whenever I saw him, my heart pounded and I turned into a quivering blob of pudding. But in a good way. It feels good to fall for someone. You'll see."

"If you say so," Leedy said, trying to sound indifferent. "And you're cute when you get all squishy."

Brittany shook her finger at Leedy. "Fine," she grumbled. "Don't believe me. You'll just have to see for yourself. Just promise me one thing."

"What's that?"

"Promise me that you will enjoy it, Leedy. It's going to be a wonderful ride."

"Oh, mush!" Leedy said, rolling her eyes. "Aren't you getting a little carried away, Brit?"

"No," Brittany said. "I'm not the one getting carried away. I've already been carried away. Now it's your turn."

Leedy wrinkled her nose at her, but she liked the sound of that phrase—*your turn.* "Oh, stop."

"No! You have a major thing for this good-looking, intelligent, charming, considerate . . . oh, and did I mention he has a nice butt . . . banker."

"You forgot to mention his butt," Leedy said. "Not that I've noticed . . ."

"Yeah, right!"

"Come on, Brit," Leedy said. "Terry hardly knows me. I just met him a few weeks ago."

"That doesn't matter."

"You're adorable. But you have wedding bells on the brain. And the banker isn't romantically interested in me. Besides, he's my class instructor and my former loan officer."

"So what?" Brittany said. "When two people are attracted to each other, they find a way to make it work. . Besides, a little bit of romance is nice too."

"I don't have time for romance."

"You don't mean that," Brittany argued. "You haven't had a date in too long! And it's been almost a year since you and Brian broke up."

The sound of Brian's name brought Leedy back to reality, and her stomach dropped at the thought of her ex-boyfriend. "Thanks for reminding me, Brit," she groaned. "But between my job here at Mr. Hobo's, the night class, and trying to open my own restaurant, I'm so busy. Maybe after my career is more on track, I would like to see more of Terry, but . . ."

"We'll see," Brittany said, her eyes twinkling. "But, don't mind me, I have wedding bells on my brain."

"Yes, you do," Leedy said. "But we better get back to work." She fake punched Brittany's shoulder and then went to the back of the kitchen and began to prepare some rolls for the dinner crowd. She spent the next hour working through her thoughts as she kneaded the soft, buttery dough.

"I'm sorry," Brittany said, standing next to the long stainless steel table where Leedy was elbow-deep in her work.

"For what?"

"I shouldn't meddle in your business."

"You weren't meddling."

"It's none of my business," she said. "And you're my boss . . . but you're my friend too." Brittany gave her a hug and Leedy returned it.

"Forget about it, Brit," Leedy said. "You can say anything to me."

"Thanks, buddy," Brittany said and she started to head out the door. She stopped, snapped her fingers and said, "Yikes! I almost forgot. I came back here to tell you that there's a lady in the dining room asking for you."

"Who is she?"

"I don't know, but I don't think she's a customer. I asked her if I could help her, but she said she'd wait for you."

Leedy washed her hands, wiped as much flour from her black tuxedo as possible, and headed for the dining room wondering who on Earth wanted to see her.

"I'm sorry to bother you at work," the dark-haired woman standing outside the big stainless steel swinging doors said. "I'm Jo Anne Phillips . . . from class. Terry Foster suggested I speak with you."

"Of course . . . Jo Anne!" Leedy said, recovering. "It's great to see you again. I'm sorry I didn't recognize you right away. My mind was a hundred miles away."

"That's quite all right."

"I've been meaning to talk with you, too," Leedy said. "It's been hectic here the past few days."

Jo Anne nodded. "I know," she said. "I wanted to catch you before class, but I've already missed one class and I was late for the other two. I was hoping we could get together and talk. It would be wonderful to have a conversation with someone who understands the difficulty involved with breaking into the restaurant business."

"I would like that very much," Leedy agreed.

Jo Anne Phillips looked to be in her late forties. She had short, curly brown hair and warm grey eyes. She was petite and slim and wore lemon yellow linen overalls over a bright orange long-sleeved T-shirt. There was a liveliness to her Leedy noticed right away—a kind of hyper-energy and confidence that belied her small size. She suspected that Jo Anne was a fireball and capable of accomplishing any task she set her mind to and she instantly took a liking to her.

"I was hoping you might be free for dinner . . . on me, of course," Jo Anne suggested. "I would love to spend some time talking with a kindred spirit. Can we get together?"

"I'd love to," Leedy said. "And I insist on treating. But I don't know how much help I could be to you. My efforts, so far, haven't been what you'd call a success. I'm no closer to opening up my restaurant than I was five years ago."

"We'll go dutch for dinner, and it looks as though you

are running this restaurant just fine," Jo Anne swept her hand to illustrate the crowded dining room. "Are you free one night this week? Wait . . . I have football and soccer practice to attend just about every night. This is why I'm having such a hard time making it to class! Could we make it Saturday?"

"Saturday is fine. I'm working the early shift."

"Wonderful," Jo Anne said. "There's an Italian restaurant on the corner of Market and King Streets. It's a lovely place called Antonio's. Not that this restaurant isn't charming, dear. I'm only assuming you may want a change of pace."

"And how." Leedy sighed, and Jo Anne smiled knowingly.

"I managed a restaurant just like this years ago," Jo Anne confided. "Coming in here, it was all I could do to keep from barking out orders as I passed the kitchen doors."

"If you see anything amiss, you go right ahead."

"I might, just for old time's sake. Is seven o'clock good for you?"

"Seven o'clock is perfect."

"Very good then," Jo Anne said, shaking Leedy's hand. "I'll see you then." She smiled another ear-to-ear grin and walked away.

"Who's that?" Brittany asked, as Jo Anne bounced past her.

"One of my new classmates," Leedy explained. "Her name is Jo Anne Phillips and she's interested in opening up a restaurant too. We're going to meet for dinner and compare war stories."

"That sounds like a wonderful idea," exclaimed Brittany. "It will do you good to talk to someone who shares your dream."

"I think so, too," Leedy said. "Although Jo Anne may be my competition someday . . ."

"Maybe," Brittany said. "Or she could become a good friend."

Chapter Seven

Leedy was deep in thought as she headed for the mall. For someone who crammed as much as she could into every minute of every day, her time in the classroom suddenly seemed woefully inadequate. Last night's class had zipped past her. Not only was she unable to talk to Jo Anne after class, Terry had slipped from the room with only a polite wave and a smile. Leedy was disappointed as all get out that he hadn't walked her to her car, but . . .

She shrugged it off. There was no point in letting small disappointments throw off her groove. It was her day off! A rare occurrence indeed, and she planned to make the most of it. She drove to the mall, all the while fretting over the fact that no one at Mr. Hobo's could prepare Chocolate Ecstasy Cakes properly. Oh, and there was that stack of resumes for a new assistant chef still sitting on her desk, waiting to be reviewed. Perhaps just a quick trip to the mall was all she needed. Then she might pop into Mr. Hobo's, just to see how things were going.

It was a sunny Wednesday afternoon and, except for a few college kids, Leedy had the mall to herself. She needed to go to the kitchen shop and buy a new sauté skillet and then she would pursue her never-ending search for shoes that were both comfortable and attractive. It had been ages since she had roamed a mall. She resisted the impulse to stop at the coffee bar for a latté. Maybe on her way out she would stop.

"Leedy?" a feminine voice from behind her called. "Is that you?"

"Yes?" she said, turning around. There behind her was a tall young woman whom she immediately recognized.

"Do you remember me?" Deanna asked. "We ran together in the race? You know my uncle?" She was wearing hip-hugging bell bottom blue jeans and a gray rag sweater that Leedy suspected had been borrowed from Terry's closet. She also carried a heavy bookbag on her back.

"Of course I remember you, Deanna!" Leedy exclaimed, not trying to hide her pleasure at seeing the cute teenager. "It's good to see you again. How are you?"

"Good," she said. "I didn't have any classes this afternoon so I'm shopping for shoes."

Leedy smiled, remembering the forlorn, puzzled expression on Terry's face the last time Deanna shopped for shoes. "Me too," Leedy confessed.

"I was just headed for Crazy Joe's Shoe Shack. I hear there's a big sale. Would you like to join me?"

Leedy couldn't think of anything else she would rather do. "I would love to," she said and they headed down the mall together.

The shoe store was just as slow as the rest of the mall— and it was a good thing too. There was a buy-one-pair, get-one-pair-free sale, and the sight of the racks of shoes made the palms of Leedy's hands sweat. "Is this heaven, or what?" she asked, and Deanna nodded in delighted agreement.

They spent the next two hours in the store, trying on pair after pair of shoes until they were both certain they had driven the clerk insane.

"Those are cute on you," Leedy said.

"They're dreamy looking, but they pinch my toes," Deanna responded.

"I can't wear high heels anymore," Leedy sighed. "I wish I could, but with my job . . . I'm always on my feet. I have to be practical."

"What about those purple sling-backs with the stiletto heels? They don't look very practical to me."

"I'm going to a wedding next month. I bought this dress that's to die for. These shoes will be a perfect match!"

It felt good to giggle with someone and Leedy wondered how long it had been since she had spent time with a female friend. While she was dating Brian, she had been part of an active social circle. But after the break-up, it had seemed too awkward to continue seeing the same group of friends as he did. Especially with Angela now in the thick of things. There was Brittany, of course, but between their mutual jobs, classes, and Brittany's long list of wedding chores, it had been months since Leedy had gone out with a friend just for the fun of it.

She was enjoying herself as much as if she were out with her best chums from high school. Deanna was funny and animated and when Leedy looked at her, it was as if she was seeing herself when she was nineteen years old.

"How many pairs are you getting?" Deanna asked.

"Well . . . six," Leedy said. "But they're on sale and it's been quite a while since I shopped for shoes."

"I know! I know!" Deanna exclaimed.

"How many pairs are you getting?" Leedy asked.

"Eight."

"Eight! Wow! I'm glad I'm not a shoe nut like you," Leedy teased.

"But I need every pair," she protested. "One pair is for school and I needed a new pair of running shoes. And even Uncle Terry says my old clogs are looking beat . . ."

"What about those lime green dancing shoes?" Leedy echoed. "They don't look very practical to me."

"But they're so pretty," Deanna said. "And they make my big feet look smaller. And since it is a buy-one-get-one-free sale, I'm really only buying four pairs of shoes, right?" She stuck her lower lip out in an adorable pout, heartbroken by the injustice of it all. Leedy wondered how Terry ever said no to her.

"I guess I'll put the lime green dancing shoes back," she sighed. "I already have a pair almost exactly like them in blue . . . and maybe I'll put back the platforms too. They are a bit frivolous. Then I'll only be getting six pairs! You're getting six pairs. That's not that many, is it?"

Leedy laughed. The kid obviously had a monkey on her back, but it was a monkey Leedy was intimately familiar with. "It sounds perfectly reasonable to me," she said. "But how is your uncle going to feel about it?"

"He doesn't have to know," Deanna said, a sly grin suddenly appearing on her face.

"I won't tell," Leedy said, smiling back. "Then it's settled. We'll both get six pairs of shoes. And I don't mind saying, I'm exhausted. I need a pick-me-up. Would you like a latté?"

"How about lunch first?" she suggested. "I'm starved."

They went to the food court where Leedy treated Deanna to soda and a pepperoni pizza with extra cheese. They found a table in a far corner of the gymnasium-like dining room.

"How is school?" Leedy asked after they were seated.

"Good," Deanna said. "Actually, it has been a breeze. Everyone gets you so psyched up about going off to college. It's turning out to be a cinch. Well, so far anyway. I'll see how my midterms go."

"You'll do just fine," she said. "Your uncle tells me you're a very bright young lady."

Deanna rolled her eyes. "He tells everyone that."

"Well, obviously, he's right. He said you're studying to be a teacher?"

"Yep," she said. "I've always wanted to teach. Ever since I was a kid myself. It would be thrilling to be in charge of a group of kids. You know . . . I can mold their young minds and help make it a better world."

"What grade would you like to teach?"

"The middle school grades," Deanna said. "I'm majoring in secondary education. I know what you're thinking. It is the scariest group of all and probably the most difficult to handle. But it is also a great time to come into a person's life. A lot of kids need extra help in middle school. I know, I was a mess when I was that age."

Leedy did the math and realized Deanna had good reason to be a mess when she was in middle school. "Were you rebellious?" she asked.

"No, at least not at school," Deanna said. "But I was

very unhappy. And confused. It was a horrible time in my life."

"I'm sorry," Leedy said.

"It's okay now," she added, smiling bravely. "Uncle Terry got me through it."

Her young face clouded for a moment and Leedy patted her hand. "You'll be a great teacher, Deanna. I wish I had a teacher with your compassion when I was in middle school. I was a bit of a mess myself."

Deanna smiled and then quickly changed the subject. She spoke in the rapid-fire fashion common among most of the teenage girls Leedy had known. As if there were too many words to say in too little time. Deanna talked about shoes and the fickle trends in foot fashion. Then they talked about her classes and life in the college dorm.

"Have you met any boys?" Leedy asked. They had finished the pizza and had finally made their way to the coffee bar. She ordered her usual vanilla latté and watched in frank admiration when Deanna ordered the largest caramel frappuccino she had ever seen.

"A few," Deanna said, sticking her tongue out and tasting the mound of whipped cream. "But don't tell Uncle Terry. He'll have a cow!"

"No! Is he strict?"

"Are you kidding?" Deanna exclaimed. "He didn't let me go on a car date until I turned seventeen! And my curfew was midnight until I graduated from high school! All my friends got to stay out until at least one o'clock. You should have seen the fuss he made when I told him I wanted to live on campus!"

"Oh?"

"He said we lived close enough to the campus for me to commute."

"Well, it is right here in Madison."

"I know, but I wanted to experience college life. It was months before he finally agreed to let me go, but he still worries. You know how he is."

"No," Leedy said. "Actually I only recently met your uncle."

"Oh!" Deanna said, and Leedy heard a tinge of wonder in her voice. "He knew you when we saw you at Mr. Hobo's, and you both seemed so . . . compatible at the race that day. You guys seemed as if you were old friends. I thought you had known him for awhile."

"No," Leedy said. "I had the pleasure of meeting your uncle for the first time only three weeks ago. He was the loan officer for a business transaction I had with his bank."

"Oh," Deanna said and paused. "You should get to know him better," she said after a moment. "You will like him. He's kind of a screwball sometimes, but he's a good guy. And some women think he's . . . okay looking . . . for an older guy, that is."

"How old is he?" Leedy asked. "I thought he was about my age."

"Sorry," Deanna said. "I didn't mean to imply that you're old, Leedy. Uncle Terry is way older than you. He's twenty-nine! Almost thirty."

"That old?" Leedy said, with feigned horror.

"Sorry," Deanna said. "I guess that isn't very old. But he seems older to me. I think of him . . . um . . . kind of like a dad. How old are you? If you don't mind telling me, that is!"

"I'm twenty-seven," Leedy said. "Almost twenty-eight."

Deanna smiled, delighted. "That isn't so bad," she said. "Much better than thirty. Do you have a boyfriend?"

"No," Leedy said, not minding that the conversation had turned more personal. If she could ask Deanna about boys, why couldn't Deanna ask her?

"How come? You're so pretty!"

"Thank you," Leedy said. "I date occasionally, but my job keeps me busy. And I'm happy with my life the way it is. Besides, boys aren't everything, are they?"

"I agree one hundred percent," Deanna admitted. "Boys are not everything. But they do keep things interesting sometimes."

"True," Leedy nodded. "They're good for that much, I suppose."

"Uncle Terry says you're trying to open a restaurant."

"Yes."

"He told me it's going to be a wonderful place. He said he'd take me there when it opens."

"Your Uncle Terry sounds quite sure of me," Leedy said, surprised. "I wish I had his confidence, and I hope he's right."

"If Uncle Terry says your restaurant will be wonderful, it will be wonderful," Deanna said. "He has a good head for business." She suddenly looked at her watch. "Oh, no!" she gasped, jumping from her seat. "I should have been home an hour ago! Uncle Terry and I have dinner together every Wednesday. He's probably worrying about me!"

"I have my cell phone. Do you want to call him?"

"No," Deanna said. "If I can just get to the bus stop and . . ."

"I'll give you a ride home."

"Oh, would you?" Deanna cried. "Freshmen are not allowed to have cars. It's such a drag. I have to keep mine at home. Are you sure it wouldn't be too much trouble?"

"Not at all," Leedy said. "I'll get you home in a jiffy. You can call your uncle from the car."

Chapter Eight

The ride from the mall to Terry's house took only ten minutes and Deanna had been right about her uncle being worried. Although Deanna had called him from Leedy's car, he was standing on the front porch with both hands shoved deeply into his pockets when they pulled up.

"There you are!" Terry scolded Deanna as she climbed out of the car, a worried expression on his face.

"I'm sorry, Uncle Terry," she said. "I was shopping with Leedy and we lost all track of the time."

"I can see that," he said. "But you and I had a dinner date, did we not?"

"Yes," she said. "We did. And I'm sorry to have kept you waiting."

"It was my fault that Deanna's late," Leedy said, climbing out of her Jeep. "I kept her longer than she would have stayed. The time got away from us."

Terry gave Leedy a secret wink when Deanna wasn't looking. "I doubt that it took much persuading on your part to keep Deanna at the shops," he said. "And, judging from the number of bags in the back seat, you two had a busy day."

"There was a sale," Deanna said. "And Leedy bought just as many pairs as I did."

Leedy's face reddened. "Well . . . uh . . . I . . ."

"Are all women crazy for shoes?" Terry asked, befuddled. "I own four pairs of shoes, and I get along just fine."

"Not all women," Leedy said. "But, yes, some women have a passion for shoes. I, on the other hand, am more practical."

"I'm sure you are," he said. He had a look in his eye, as if he wanted to say more, then he remembered Deanna was standing next to him. He wagged his finger at her. "Well, young lady," he said. "You're home, safe and sound, and at least you had the good sense to call me from Leedy's car." He then playfully punched her on the shoulder and tousled her hair. "And since you brought a beautiful woman home with you, you're back in my good graces. This time! But next time I expect you to be here at the designated time, understand?"

"I understand," Deanna giggled. "Did anyone call?"

"Some boy named Chris," he said. "Who's Chris? Have I met him?" But Deanna had already dashed into the house.

Terry jerked his thumb at her and then looked at Leedy helplessly. "Help me," he said. "Stay and have dinner with us."

Leedy looked at her watch. She had planned on stopping by Mr. Hobo's, but now it suddenly seemed unnecessary. "I suppose I have a few minutes to spare," she said. "And I'm a little bit hungry . . ."

"Great," he said. "Come on in."

He led the way through the front door, and Leedy was immediately struck by how well the house suited him. It was a pale yellow Cape Cod nestled on a quiet street in an old but well-maintained neighborhood. The house itself was small, and except for the multitudes of pictures of Deanna in all stages of her childhood, it had the unmistakable feel of a male's presence. The furnishings were minimal. There was a black leather sofa in the living room, along with some Scandinavian-styled tables. A shelf that squatted against the wall held an impressive stereo and television system. A big picture window that overlooked the front yard had fat wooden blinds but no curtains. The house was masculine except for some scattered decorations Leedy sensed had been added for Deanna's benefit. A stack of denim floor pillows were piled in a corner of the room in case teenagers stopped by. There was also a large framed photograph of a daisy and a few scattered pencil sketches on the walls. The fireplace mantle was full of basketball and swimming trophies.

"This is very nice," Leedy said, and she meant it. Terry's house was as comfortable and relaxed as the family that lived there.

"Thanks," he said.

"I'll give you the grand tour," Deanna said, appearing from the kitchen. She took Leedy's hand and led her down the hallway. She showed her the house while Terry went to the kitchen to fix them all drinks.

As Leedy suspected, the rest of the house was much the same decor as the living room. Except for Deanna's room, which was decorated in pastel blues and purples with strings of plastic beads in the windows and a beanbag chair in the corner.

"This is Uncle Terry's room," Deanna said, taking Leedy into the furthest room in the hallway and lingering there. His bedroom was bigger than Deanna's, but not by much. Still, it was also remarkably neat and held an expensive bedroom suite. Leedy hoped she would somehow be provided with more insight into the man who occupied the room that smelled faintly of his aftershave. Leedy was happy to see that there was no sign of feminine influence, other than more photographs of Deanna that were strategically placed around the room.

"This is nice," she commented. "And so clean."

"Did you expect piles of underwear on the floor?" Terry asked. He had caught up to them, holding two glasses of iced tea.

"There are in my apartment," she joked. There were not, of course, but she found his neatness endearing and she couldn't resist poking at him.

"I'd like to see that," Terry said softly as he handed her the glass. "Remind me to stop by unannounced one day. What would you two like for dinner? I could call in a pizza . . ."

Deanna and Leedy looked at each other and laughed. "How about Chinese food tonight, Uncle Terry?" Deanna asked. "Leedy and I had pizza for lunch."

"Chinese food sounds good to me," he said. "I rented an Arnold Schwarzenegger movie. We could . . ." He stopped in mid-sentence and eyed his niece suspiciously. "Do you have homework?" he asked, his eyes narrowing.

"I did most of it earlier."

"Most of it?"

"I just have a little reading to do," Deanna said. "But I don't have to . . ."

"You better get to it then," he said, his eyebrows raised. "I'll order from Lee's Flying Wok and Leedy and I will go out on the patio so that you will not be disturbed. You can take a break from your homework when the food gets here."

Deanna groaned but went to her bedroom, dragging the bookbag she had worn on her back most of the day. "Okay, okay," she grumbled. "But there better be some egg rolls left when I come out."

Terry led Leedy out to the back yard. There was a stone patio and a small wrought iron table and chairs. The landscaping was as neat and uncluttered as the house. The lawn was mowed and there was a small garden.

"Is it too chilly out here for you?" he asked. "I could put on a pot of coffee if you're cold."

"No," Leedy said. "The iced tea is fine."

She supposed she should feel out of place, coming to this house and sitting on this patio sipping tea. After all, the house belonged to a man who was practically a stranger. But somehow she didn't feel at all uncomfortable. Somehow Terry's house felt as cozy to her as her own place. And somehow, sitting outside with him in his yard sipping iced tea was as easy as slipping on a well-worn, flannel robe.

"Thanks again for bringing Deanna home," he said after they had settled down across from one another at the table. "She talks a big game, but I think college is a big adjustment for her. I'm sure a day of shopping with you did her a lot of good."

"I don't know about her," Leedy said. "But it was good for me. I had a great time at the mall with her. It was like a day out with one of my old friends. She's a great kid."

"I think so, too," he said. "But I may be biased. Not everyone takes time out for teenagers, and Deanna needs special attention sometimes. Thank you again."

"Don't mention it," Leedy said, taking another sip of her drink. "It was my pleasure."

"And I'm glad you came here," he said, looking at her with an expectant, longing look in his eyes. She fell into the gaze almost immediately, as if she was drowning in his eyes.

"You're home early, aren't you?" she said, at last. "I thought you would still be at your desk working out new ways to foreclose on some poor little old lady's home."

"I slip out early every Wednesday," Terry said. "I meet Deanna here and we have dinner together. Besides, I handle commercial loans, not residential. A woman by the name of Paula Jefferson handles the little old lady foreclosures."

The sun was quickly slipping down into the sky, and their conversation stalled as they watched the end of the day. The effect of the sunset cast a strange shadow over the patio. It held a soft, pink warmth that floated over her. It gave her a soft, dreamlike feeling and filled her with a sense of anticipation and delight. The soft colors played across the sky as dusk approached. It also did wonders for the color of Terry's eyes. They seemed to almost glow in their blueness. Leedy felt a gentle stirring within her, a stirring that was becoming all too familiar when she was near him. A feeling of longing and awe and desire all at the same time.

"You look very pretty in this light," he said, his voice dropping to almost a whisper. "But then again, you look pretty in any light."

"Thank you," she said. "You're making me blush."

"I'm sorry," he said. "I can't help it. I find you attractive, Leedy. Very attractive . . ."

She said nothing. She found him attractive too, of course, but she did not know how to tell him. He was watching her with a new expression on his face. An expression that hinted there was more he wanted to say. An expression of breathless desire and aching passion. It was a look that warmed her all the way down to her toes and made the butterflies in her stomach take flight all over again.

He leaned across the table and brushed a loose hair back into place. "You have the most beautiful hair I've ever seen," he said in a hoarse voice. "It's so soft and shiny. It's like silk." Leedy still said nothing, but the sound of his deep, sexy voice was sending shivers up her spine. She looked into his face and was immediately lost again in his blue, blue eyes. Her heart was pounding and her breathing was uneven.

"Leedy . . . I . . ." he began. "You're absolutely gorgeous and . . ."

She thought she heard the sound of a doorbell from far away and then, before Terry could finish his sentence, Deanna was calling them from inside the house.

"The food is here, Uncle Terry!" she shouted as she yanked open the sliding glass door. "Cough up some cash for the delivery guy! And I get first dibs on the Egg Foo Young."

Terry blinked his eyes and then shook his head. "Rotten kid," he whispered to Leedy. "She sure knows how to kill a moment. Remind me to tell her that she's grounded."

"I guess we better go in," Leedy said, her voice shaking.

They reluctantly went into the house. Terry pointed Leedy to the kitchen, then excused himself to pay for their dinner. She found Deanna setting the table. She had already piled the food cartons onto a lazy Susan that sat in the middle of the table and was now laying out chopsticks and napkins.

"Oops," Deanna said when Terry reappeared, looking dazed. She gave him a look of apology. "I hope I didn't interrupt . . ."

"That's okay," Leedy said. "We were just watching the sunset."

"It was beautiful," he said, looking at her. Then he remembered Deanna. "You must be starving, kiddo. I know what an appetite all that shoe shopping can create." He pulled a chair out for his niece and then for Leedy. He lightly touched her elbow as she sat down. His hand was gentle against her skin, but underneath the pressure, she felt a tremble to his touch.

Deanna piled food on Leedy's plate, but she barely noticed. She couldn't stop thinking about Terry on the patio . . . and the way his fingertips felt against her skin. No one had ever touched her that way. No one had ever made her feel like this.

Deanna was telling Terry about their day. She had a way of speaking that was rational and dramatic all at the same time. She told him about the shoe store and the rows of "way sweet" shoes she had stopped herself from buying. She also told him all about lunch with Leedy and how it was the most fun she had since last May's spring break.

"I had fun too," Leedy said. "We have to do it again soon."

"Okay," Deanna said, excited. "How about next Wednesday?"

"Deanna," Terry scolded.

"Wednesday is good," Leedy said. The words came out too quickly and for a moment she felt ashamed of herself. She didn't want Deanna to think she was trying to get to Terry by forming a relationship with her. Which she would never do!

Would she?

No. Of course not. She was genuinely fond of Deanna. There was a quality to the girl that was captivating. She had touched a spot in Leedy that she had not realized existed. Leedy felt an almost overpowering need to take care of Deanna. To mother her.

"Great," Deanna said. "Can you meet me at the coffee bar? Let's say noon."

"Sounds good to me," Leedy said, smiling broadly.

"Try to keep her out of the shoe stores," Terry said. "But what am I saying? It's like sending the wolf in to guard the hen house, isn't it?"

"I'll try to control myself," Leedy said.

They talked and laughed and dawdled over dinner. Terry made a pot of decaffeinated coffee and they sat around the kitchen table, telling stories and drinking the whole pot.

"Oh my gosh!" Deanna said, suddenly jumping out of her seat. "It's after nine o'clock! I'm late! I gotta get back to the dorm!"

"Late for what?" he asked. "What's your hurry? You don't have an early class tomorrow. I thought we were going to watch the movie?"

"I'm sorry, Uncle Terry," Deanna said. "But I've got a ton of homework left to do!"

"But I thought you said you only had a little reading."

"It's more than I thought. . . . Can you give me a lift?"

"I can give you a ride," Leedy offered, getting up from the chair. "I should be leaving myself."

"I'll drive her," Terry said, a note of disappointment in his voice. "And you could come with me. Then we could come back here and watch the movie . . . if you'd like?"

Leedy almost accepted the offer, but just then the telephone on the wall began to ring. He answered it, absent-mindedly. "Hello," he said, distracted. "Oh . . . um . . . hi."

Something had changed in the tone of his voice that made Leedy's ears perk up. She didn't know who was on the other end of the phone, but whoever it was had a visible effect on him.

"No," he said, his voice dropping to a low murmur. "Not tonight. Deanna's here and we're . . . fine. Tomorrow would be better." He hung up the phone and looked at Deanna and then at Leedy. He then smiled warily. "Work," he said, with an unconvincing shrug. "They don't know when to call it a day sometimes."

Terry had a look on his face that Leedy immediately recognized from her last few months with Brian. It was the same look of deception and guilt that she had told herself was only her imagination.

"I better be going," she said, pasting a smile on her face.

"Are you sure you wouldn't like to watch the movie?" he offered. "You can stay here, if you'd like. I'll take Deanna back to her dorm and be back here in no time . . ."

"I have to work tomorrow," she said. "I better not." It was true she had to work the lunch shift at Mr. Hobo's the next day. But she didn't have to be there until ten o'clock. She endured the tempting image of spending the evening curled up on the sofa watching an action movie with Terry. But the effect of the phone call determined her decision.

"No, thank you."

"Okay," he said. "But I don't want to impose on you. I'll take Deanna back to her dorm."

"It's no trouble," she said. "In fact, it's right on the way. It will give me the chance to thank her for the shopping trip."

Deanna appeared carrying her bookbag, and Leedy bade a quick goodbye to Terry at the front door. "See you in class tomorrow, Professor," she said. "And thanks for a lovely dinner."

Deanna was bouncing from foot to foot, obviously in a hurry to get into the car. "Bye, Uncle T," she said, giving him a quick peck on the cheek. "I'll see you Saturday morning!"

"Saturday morning?" Terry asked. "I thought you'd be coming home Friday night?"

"I have a date," Deanna said, bounding down the steps. Leedy followed behind her.

"A date?" he frowned. "All right. But don't stay out too late, Dee. And I'll see you on Saturday. Leedy . . . thanks again. I'll see you tomorrow in class. Maybe we can go out afterwards for coffee?"

Leedy did not say anything, but instead headed for the driveway. Deanna was already in the car with her seatbelt on waiting expectantly for the ride to take her back to her dorm. Leedy started the engine, gave one final wave to Terry and headed into the night, with Deanna all but spinning in the passenger's seat next to her.

"Turn left at the stop sign," she said. "I know a shortcut."

Deanna chattered nervously the whole way back to the college campus. She faked a yawn and smiled but every few moments she would glance anxiously at her watch.

"What's his name?" Leedy asked, as they turned into the University's entrance.

Deanna hesitated for a second. "Chris," she said. "Am I that obvious?"

"Only to the trained eye," Leedy said. "Where are you and Chris going?"

"We'll probably just watch television with some friends," Deanna said. "I told him I would be home by nine o'clock though. As usual, I'm late."

"Only by a half-hour," Leedy said, pulling up to the building Deanna had led her to.

"Thanks," she said, climbing out of the car. "I had a lot of fun today, Leedy. And I'm glad I got to know you better."

"Me, too," Leedy said, and she meant it.

"Um . . . Leedy?"

"Yes?"

"Don't tell Uncle Terry about Chris, okay?"

"He already knows you date, doesn't he?"

"Well, yes," Deanna said, as she looked at the building and then back at Leedy. "But . . ."

"But, what?"

"Nothing," she said, a sigh in her voice. "I just wish Uncle Terry would go out more. Then he wouldn't worry about me so much."

Leedy nodded in understanding. But she understood Terry just as much, if not more. It certainly couldn't be easy on him to send his pretty niece off to college. Leedy watched Deanna dash up the steps into the dormitory building. She thought she saw a tall, blonde-haired boy in a black jacket walk up and greet her at the door, but she was not sure if it was an embrace or simply a welcome between fellow students. Leedy tilted her head to one side, watching the couple. It was probably her imagination, but there was something familiar about the boy.

She shrugged and pulled away from the curb. "Ah," she sighed to the empty car. "Young love . . ." She drove away, thinking about romance. But more than Deanna and Chris, she thought about a handsome blue-eyed man who was watching a movie alone in his living room. "I wonder who that phone call was from," Leedy said out loud. It was all she could do to keep from driving back to his house.

Chapter Nine

Leedy had heard that the restaurant Antonio's was a wonderful place to eat, but since most of her evenings were devoted to Mr. Hobo's, she had not yet been there. She arrived right on time to find Jo Anne already waiting for her when she walked through the door. Jo Anne was wearing an attractive long, black silk dress with a coordinating long, black floral jacket. She looked every bit the picture of a poised and sophisticated woman about town.

"I'm over here," Jo Anne called, waving. Leedy walked over and gave Jo Anne a warm hug. "Antonio's is usually packed by this time, so I came a little early," Jo Anne confided. "Our table is ready. It's in the back."

The hostess led the way as Jo Anne and Leedy followed her through the restaurant. They could smell the wonderful aromas as they passed by the kitchen doors, which reminded Leedy that she had not eaten anything since breakfast.

"I'm starved," she confessed when they were seated in

a corner table near a window. They had a nice view of the courtyard behind Antonio's.

"I remember those days of working in a restaurant and skipping lunch," Jo Anne said. "Ironic, isn't it? Always being surrounded by delicious food, yet somehow you can never find the time to eat."

"Yes," Leedy said. "When I was a chef in California, I ate all the time. If only to make sure the food tasted good. Now, all I can manage is a quick snack in the dish room. I hardly ever sit down and eat a real meal."

"You're a chef too?" Jo Anne said. "Terry didn't mention that."

"Yes," Leedy said. "I attended the Cornwell Institute and apprenticed in a few restaurants in Southern California."

"How exciting!"

"It was fun, in a crazy, exhausting way. But I only did it for a few years. I also worked for a small catering company."

"What brought you to Mr. Hobo's?" Jo Anne asked.

"I wanted to come back home to Wisconsin. I grew up just outside of Madison. I also wanted to learn the ropes of running a restaurant. When the manager's job opened up at Mr. Hobo's, I took it. I thought it would give me some insight into the management side of the restaurant business."

"Has it?" Jo Anne asked.

"Yes," Leedy said. "Managing a restaurant is a lot tougher than I thought it would be. I always thought the kitchen was the only part of the place that was in constant chaos. Now I know better."

"Oh, yes," Jo Anne said. "The restaurant business is a difficult industry."

"Tell me about it."

"What types of foods do you cook?" Jo Anne asked.

"Italian cuisine is my favorite," Leedy said, nodding at the menu. "Particularly recipes with lots of garlic and tomatoes. My personal favorites are anything with seafood. My grandmother was from Sicily and I have some wonderful old family recipes. How about you? What is your background?"

"I never was formally trained," Jo Anne said, "but I grew up in the restaurant business. My father had a deli in Philadelphia. I could make a cheesesteak before I could ride a bike. My father retired years ago, but the deli is still in the family. My youngest brother runs it now. It has become even more popular than when my father owned it. Roger is doing quite well. It was recently voted best cheap eats in town by the local newspaper."

"It sounds like my favorite kind of deli," Leedy noted. "I don't care much for the chains."

"I agree. I miss Philly sometimes, although I love Madison. I visit with my family a few times a year though, and I always stop by the old place. It still has the best hot pastrami on rye I've ever tasted."

"Do you cook?" Leedy asked.

"Yes," Jo Anne said. "I love to cook, and I'm a really good baker, even if I do say so myself. Especially anything to do with chocolate. Chocolate cheesecake, chocolate silk pie, homemade chocolate-covered toffees . . ."

"Mmm," Leedy said. "I think we should definitely get dessert after dinner. Don't you?"

"I was hoping you would say that."

They picked up their menus and read the offerings with keen interest, commenting on possible spices used to prepare this or cooking techniques used to prepare that. They chit-chatted about their lives, and Leedy felt instantly comfortable talking with the friendly, likeable woman she had just met. As a matter of fact, by the time the waitress had taken their dinner orders, she felt as if she and Jo Anne were old friends.

"Tell me about your restaurant," she said.

"Which restaurant is that, dear?" Jo Anne asked.

"You know which restaurant. *Your* restaurant. The one you would open tomorrow if you could."

"Oh, that restaurant," Jo Anne said and smiled wistfully. "It has been an ambition I've had for many years, you know. Even when I was a teenager working the counter of my father's deli, I couldn't imagine ever doing any other kind of work. I had already decided the restaurant business was as natural to me as breathing, but I thought a young lady of my sophistication was destined for a finer establishment."

Jo Anne gave the impression that she was teasing, but Leedy knew better. She knew that Jo Anne's restaurant was as real to her as Leedy's restaurant was to her. And both places were as real as the restaurant they were sitting in. "It will be elegant," Jo Anne began. "But not in the snooty, intimidating way some places I've been to have been. My restaurant will be classy, but in a warm, inviting way. I'll furnish it in a traditional decor. You know, lots of cherry wood and starched linens. It will also serve the finest gourmet menu in Wisconsin. In fact, if you didn't already have other ambitions, I'd want someone like you to be the chef. Someone with formal training and a diverse background. My restaurant would be located inside the city, or, alternatively, just barely outside the city limits. But not too far away as to make it inconvenient to my customers. Oh, and there would be a huge room for private banquets. I love planning big parties, especially wedding receptions. I'm good at it, too. I've helped a few of my friends plan their children's weddings. Now I'm the first person anyone calls when someone gets engaged."

"I would love to have seen the receptions," Leedy said, nodding.

"I have lots of pictures. I'll show you them one day . . . if you'd like to see them. They were beautiful affairs. But, at the same time, I'm very budget-conscious. I consider it a challenge to create the nicest reception with the least amount of money. It's difficult sometimes, but I enjoy doing it. Now, tell me about your restaurant?"

"My restaurant?" Leedy said, thoughtfully. "It's funny, Jo Anne. To tell you the truth, my restaurant sounds quite similar to yours, although I had not given as much thought to a banquet room. But my place has the same feel to it. I want a state-of-the-art menu in a classic but comfortable setting. I want elegance and gourmet food in a friendly place, just like you."

"Have you thought about what you would call your place?" Jo Anne asked.

"I don't know," Leedy confided. "I thought of Leedy's House but that sounds a little bit too big-headed when I say it out loud. It needs some more work. I've also thought of naming it after something that speaks of the history of the area. How about you?"

"I would name it after my boys," Jo Anne said, decisively. "They're almost grown now, but they're still my babies. Ryan is seventeen and Riley just turned fifteen.

What do you think of the Ryan-Riley Inn? Do you think people will assume it is an Irish pub?"

"I like it," Leedy said, nodding. "And you can change the pub image through your advertising."

"That's true," Jo Anne said. "My husband is willing to dig into our savings to get this thing off the ground. But the money we've saved wouldn't be nearly enough. Especially with sending two boys off to college soon."

"I know what you mean," Leedy said. "Except for the added stress of saving for college, of course. It seems as though I've been saving for this forever, but I can barely keep up with the cost of inflation. I'm not making much progress."

The two women talked for the rest of the dinner as if they were old, dear friends. In fact, other than her shopping trip with Deanna, Leedy couldn't remember when she had enjoyed someone's company as much as Jo Anne's. They talked through dinner, then dessert, and then lingered over coffee.

"Oh, my heavens!" Jo Anne gasped, looking at her watch. "It is almost ten-thirty! I can't believe we've stayed here this late!"

"Don't you hate it when people hog a table all night?" Leedy said, just as surprised that the time had passed so quickly.

"Oh, I remember those people!" Jo Anne said, scornfully. "Now look, I've become one of them! We better leave a good tip."

"Let's double it," Leedy added, digging in her purse for her wallet.

The two women paid the check and walked out into the

parking lot. They strolled through the cold night, still deep in conversation.

"This was a wonderful evening," Jo Anne said. "I'm so glad I took Terry's suggestion and introduced myself."

"I am too," Leedy said, her ears perking up at the sound of Terry's name. "Um . . . do you know him . . . personally?"

"Oh, yes," Jo Anne said. "Terry Foster is an excellent loan officer and a wonderful friend. He helped my husband, Ted, get his dental practice off the ground years ago. As a matter of fact, he was the one who gave us the best advice of anyone we talked to, including our lawyer."

"He seems nice," Leedy said, hoping Jo Anne would tell her more.

"He's a great guy," Jo Anne said. "Smart as can be, and a wonderful father-figure to Deanna."

"I met Deanna," Leedy said and told Jo Anne about her shopping trip at the mall with the teenager. "She's a beautiful young woman. I'm deeply sorry for Deanna and Terry's loss."

"Deanna's mother was Terry's big sister," Jo Anne said. "I remember her well. A splendid woman named Colleen. Her husband was Frank McQuinn. They got caught in a snowstorm on their way home from visiting friends. A truck hit a patch of ice and . . . Well, it was a tragedy. A terrible, terrible tragedy."

Leedy thought of Deanna growing up without her mother and father and felt saddened. "Terry's done a good job with her," she said. "From all I've seen, she's a sweet, level-headed, bright young woman."

"Oh, yes," Jo Anne continued. "Deanna's doing great

now. She went through a difficult time after her parents died, though."

"That's understandable. She was a child when it happened."

"And she's still very possessive with Terry's attention."

"Oh? I didn't notice."

"Yes," Jo Anne said. "She was only twelve when her parents died. It broke Terry's heart to watch her hurting. He did everything he could to let Deanna know she was safe and protected. She finally came around. But she's still suspicious of outsiders. Especially when it comes to her uncle. She sure has given some of Terry's past girlfriends a run for their money."

"Really?" Leedy said, surprised.

"Not that Terry confides in me about his love life," Jo Anne said. "He's a very private person. But I hear things through Ted. My husband and Terry meet every week or so for lunch. They've become good friends. Terry dated a few women over the years, but Deanna never seemed to care for any of them. Of course, he never put up much of a fight when a girlfriend became angry over some shenanigan Deanna pulled. There was never any question as to where his loyalties lay."

"What did Deanna do to them?" Leedy asked, trying to imagine the sweet teenager doing anyone any harm.

"Oh, it was never anything horrible," Jo Anne said. "She would just give them dirty looks or 'forget' to give Terry their telephone messages. I think she once dumped Tabasco on one girlfriend's sandwich. And then there was the ugly rumor that she put gum in someone else's hair. I heard the poor woman had to get a crew cut."

Leedy wanted to giggle, but she caught herself. She was

liking Deanna's spunk more and more by the minute. "She must have been a lot younger when she did those things," Leedy said. "She always been so sweet since I've known her."

"I don't know about that," Jo Anne said. "The last incident I heard about was only last year. I think her name was Claire or Mare . . . something like that. Deanna ran over her foot with her mountain bike . . . or was it her car? I'm getting my information from my husband. Ted is sketchy on the details so I can't be certain. I think the foot was broken or maybe just bruised. I'm not sure."

"I can't believe Deanna would intentionally hurt someone," Leedy protested. "That doesn't sound like her."

"She might, if she thought her uncle was threatened," Jo Anne said. "She's changing her tune lately though. Since she moved to the dorms she thinks her uncle is spending too much of his time alone. Terry told Ted that Deanna has been after him to date more lately. Suddenly, Deanna *wants* Terry to meet someone. Not just any one, of course. She is quite specific about who she sees as an acceptable mate for her uncle. She does have her standards." Jo Anne stopped at a dark green mini-van. "This is mine," she said, groping into her enormous black leather feedbag of a purse for her car keys. "Ted told me Terry thinks she has a boyfriend and is afraid to tell him."

"Why would Deanna be afraid to tell him that?" Leedy asked. "She's over eighteen and I'm sure even Terry knows the campus is co-ed."

"Terry and Deanna are very close," Jo Anne said. "They've both been through a great deal of grief together and it made them closer than most uncle-niece relationships. Hell, closer than most father-daughter relationships

I know of. Ted and Terry went to lunch the other day and Terry told Ted that Deanna has someone in particular in mind she wants him to date . . . where are those stupid keys? Ted said Deanna was quite insistent with Terry. Oh, here they are."

Jo Anne unlocked the door and climbed into the van.

"And?" Leedy asked, before Jo Anne could shut the door.

"And, what?" Jo Anne asked.

"Whom did Deanna pick for her uncle?" Leedy said, trying to pretend that she was not altogether interested in the answer.

Jo Anne rolled down the window and shut the car door, as if she were settling in for a long drive instead of the ten minutes it would take her to get home. "Well, Terry Foster is the most handsome man in town so he certainly does not need Deanna's help in finding a date."

"I haven't noticed," Leedy said, shrugging indifferently.

"Oh, come on now, Leedy," Jo Anne scolded. "You're a woman, aren't you? And you still have a pulse, right? Don't pretend you haven't noticed his blue eyes! Or the broad shoulders? Or his sexy voice?"

"Well . . . er . . . I . . ."

"Men with Terry Foster's packaging are usually only found in magazines," Jo Anne said. "I can't believe you haven't noticed!"

"Okay, okay," Leedy said. "I'm not blind. Terry is . . . cute."

"Cute!"

"Yes, for a man who declined the loan application for my restaurant, cute is the best I can do."

Jo Anne laughed. "Oh, pooh," she said. "Terry declined

Ted's application the first time around too. Then he told us exactly what we needed to do to get it right. Listen to what he has to say, Leedy. He's got a good head for business matters and his advice is usually right on the money. You're just not ready yet, dear. By the way, where did you park? Can I drive you to your car?"

"I'm right there in the next row," Leedy said, pointing to her Jeep.

Jo Anne smiled and nodded. "I'll see you in class then. This was such fun. Maybe we can go out for coffee after class next week?"

"I would like that very much," Leedy said, and Jo Anne started her engine.

"Wait!" Leedy exclaimed.

"Yes?" Jo Anne asked.

"You never told me who the woman was Deanna had chosen for Terry."

"Oh, my goodness," Jo Anne said. "I thought you, of all people, already knew!"

"Knew what?"

"Why, it's you, silly," Jo Anne said. "Deanna liked you from the moment she saw you at Mr. Hobo's. You must have made quite an impression on her, dear, because Deanna has picked you to be her Uncle Terry's new girl-friend."

"Me?" Leedy gasped. "But Deanna barely knows me. We spent a day together shopping just that once but I hard-ly know her . . ."

Jo Anne shrugged and waved her hand. "Apparently that does not matter to Deanna . . . or to Terry either. I've no-ticed the way he looks at you in class, and I guess his niece did too. Deanna says you're the one."

Chapter Ten

"Terry and I are going out for a latté after class to-night," Jo Anne whispered in Leedy's ear. "Would you like to come with us?"

Thursday night's class was just starting, but Leedy had already begun hoping someone would suggest an after-class outing. Even if it was two hours away. "Okay," she said, a bit too quickly. "It's been a long week. A latté sounds like just what I need."

She stole a quick glance at the blond who sat in the front of the classroom. The woman who had been making eyes at Terry since he walked in. The same woman who made eyes at him during every class. Leedy crossed her fingers and hoped that the blond wouldn't be invited along for coffee.

Krissy Montgomery was wearing a black miniskirt and a cropped pale blue sweater that showed just a little midriff. It also had a plunging neckline. Leedy felt a pang of an-noyance when she noticed that Krissy sat in such a way as to give Terry a generous view of her cleavage. He was standing at the front of the classroom, unpacking his briefcase. Leedy noticed him give Krissy a quick smile. She even gave him extra credit for trying to keep his eyes on her face. Just then, Krissy stood up and walked around to the business side of Terry's desk, standing slightly behind him. She leaned over him and was whispering in his ear while moving closer and closer by the second.

Leedy thought of a few choice names to call Krissy, some of which included disparaging remarks about her hair color, but then she remembered Brittany and Deanna were also blond. "Except they're *real* blondes," she thought bitterly to herself. Leedy scolded herself for being catty as she watched Krissy's wiggling and giggling in front of Terry for as long as she could stand it. She shivered with disdain and opened her notebook. Surely, rereading her notes was a better use of her time.

But, deep down, Leedy couldn't blame Krissy for flaunting her assets, nor did she blame her for flirting. Didn't every other woman in the class seem to flutter around him as if they were moths on a porch light? But Krissy always seemed to take it one step further than the other women. And she didn't seem to be above using any trick in the book to get his attention, be it revealing clothes, unblushing flirtation or . . . or . . .

Leedy fumed at Krissy's choice of the classroom as a desirable location to turn up the romantic heat and she wished that, just once, Krissy would wear a turtleneck to class. But, no, she couldn't really blame Krissy, or any red-blooded woman for that matter, for being attracted to Terry Foster. Even bombshells like Krissy Montgomery are, after all, only human.

Leedy looked up from her notebook. Krissy was now sitting in her seat, looking somewhat pouty, and Terry was standing in front of the classroom. A sure sign that he was ready to begin the night's lecture. Leedy saw that he was looking at her. When he caught her eye he gave her a smile and a secret wink. She returned the smile with a dreamy one of her own.

She loved Terry's class. Every topic that he raised was one of critical relevance to her, and she was surprised at how much she had learned in the three weeks she had been there. She thought she had seen it all over the years working in the restaurant business, but sharing business war stories with the class gave her new insight into the many pitfalls of self-employment.

"Okay, group," Terry said, his eyes lingering on Leedy's side of the room. Krissy Montgomery turned around in her chair and squinted in her direction. Was it her imagination, or did Krissy Montgomery just give her a dirty look? "Tonight we're going to answer that all-important question—will *your* business be successful? Not every business succeeds, of course. But there are some guidelines to help you predict the viability of your business venture. What do I mean by that? . . . Miss Montgomery?"

Krissy smiled magnificently at him and batted her long, perfect eyelashes. "I believe you mean that someone who is looking into beginning a new business should examine all the relevant factors involved before taking those first steps. This is in hopes of objectively discerning whether or not a business will be successful."

"Right," Terry said. "Very good. Can you give me an example?"

"Yes," Krissy said, giving Leedy a sideways glare and

flipping her blonder-than-blond hair back with a haughty jerk of her head. "For instance, if I wanted to . . . let's say, open up a restaurant . . . I would need to decide on the type of restaurant I wanted to open, then choose the best location for my restaurant. I also should ask myself do I have a good feel for the community I will be serving. And even whether or not I have enough brains to follow through with a business strategy . . ." Leedy felt the hairs on the back of her neck stand on end and she glanced at Jo Anne. Jo Anne gave Krissy a warning glare; then she looked at Leedy and shrugged.

"The type of restaurant and where it will be located are important," Terry said. "And we'll assume, for the sake of argument, that there is an adequate supply of brains present. What are some other factors a new business should consider?"

"A few things that come to mind are the education and work experience required. Do I need more? For instance, a degree in business and/or a few years in the trenches would be essential."

"Good point," Terry said and Krissy beamed. Once again, Leedy noticed Krissy give her a sideways glance.

"What's with Blondie?" Jo Anne whispered to Leedy. "Is she trying to tell us something?" Leedy shook her head and rolled her eyes.

"How about start-up capital?" a man from the back of the room asked. "That has been my biggest hurdle. How much money will it take to get the business off the ground?"

"You're right about that being the biggest hurdle," Terry said. "That is a class by itself, of course, but you're absolutely right."

The class discussion turned to start-up costs and budgeting and Leedy quickly forgot about Krissy's nasty remarks. She wrote down every word Terry said and, once again, made a mental note to buy a pocket-sized tape recorder in hopes of sparing her poor, cramped hand.

The rest of the class passed all too quickly. Suddenly it was time to go and Leedy was still laboriously writing in her notebook. She looked up and saw Jo Anne smiling at her, patiently waiting for her to finish writing. Terry was in the front of the room talking with the usual harem of students, all young, female, and eager to talk with him. She felt a stab of jealousy when she saw Krissy was standing the closest, leaning in and listening to something he was saying. She was smiling, her hand lightly touching his elbow as she tried to monopolize his attention.

"Don't worry about Krissy," Jo Anne whispered. "She isn't Terry's type."

"I wasn't worried about her," Leedy said, trying to make her voice sound convincing. "I'm worried about getting to the coffee bar before it closes."

"We have plenty of time," Jo Anne said patiently.

"Good, because I'd love a vanilla latté," Leedy smiled, but her glance returned to the gaggle of students at Terry's desk. "Better make it a large."

"I said, don't worry about Krissy."

"Okay." Leedy said. "I won't. Although I'm not sure about the comments she made earlier. I'm sure she didn't mean anything personal by them, but what's up with the attitude?"

"I don't know about her attitude," Jo Anne said. "But I do know that her comments were personal . . . and they were directed to you, my dear. Krissy was trying to slam you, Leedy. Evidently, Deanna and I are not the only ones who have noticed Terry's reaction to you."

Leedy blushed. "He treats me the same way he treats every one else in the room," she scoffed.

"On the surface, yes," Jo Anne noted.

"Besides," Leedy added. "Look at her. Krissy strikes me as someone who can hold her own when she sets out to attract a man."

"Maybe she can attract other men," Jo Anne said. "But Terry hasn't shown much interest. Did you know this is the third time Krissy Montgomery has taken this class?"

"You're kidding! The third time?"

"The third time."

"No," Leedy said. "I didn't know that."

"She's been coming on to him for months now. And I can't help but point out that if Krissy hasn't set off his bells yet, she probably never will. Of course, he knows what her real intentions are."

"What real intentions?"

"I'll tell you all about it some other time. But, until then, don't worry about her, Leedy. Krissy Montgomery isn't Terry Foster's type."

Leedy wanted to press Jo Anne for more information, but she noticed Terry had finally gotten Krissy and the other women out of the classroom and was now headed their way.

"Are we ready?" he asked.

"Yes," Jo Anne said. "Leedy?"

"All set," Leedy said, trying not to look at him. She tossed her bookbag over her shoulder.

"Where would you ladies like to go?" Terry asked, leading the way.

"How about . . . Oh, no!" Jo Anne gasped, suddenly stopping. "I just remembered! I promised Ryan I would help him with his homework tonight. He has a paper for English that's due tomorrow. I told him I would type it up for him. I can't go!"

"We can all go out another night," Leedy said, feeling her stomach sink in disappointment.

"Nonsense," Jo Anne said. "I know how much you want to continue with the discussion from class. And I also know what a coffee junkie you are. Why don't you and Terry go on without me."

"Okay," Terry said before Leedy had a chance to protest. "Sounds like fun to me."

"Well . . . I don't want to keep you from anything . . ." Leedy stammered, looking at Terry shyly. The thought of being alone with him made her feel suddenly flushed.

"You're not keeping me from anything," Terry said. "Deanna has a date tonight and I don't have any plans."

Leedy shrugged. "Well, all right," she said, trying to sound nonchalant.

"Very well then," Jo Anne said. "I'll see you two on Tuesday night. Have a good weekend."

Leedy thought she detected a look of triumphant amusement on Jo Anne's face, but she was not certain. They walked Jo Anne to her mini-van and said a quick goodbye.

"Good luck with the English paper," Terry said. "Don't let Ryan get you to write it for him. I fell for that one once."

"I'm just the typist," Jo Anne assured him. "He better have the thing written by the time I get there. See you two later!"

"Drive safely," Leedy called, and just as quickly as Jo

Anne had gotten into her car, she found herself standing alone with Terry.

"Have you eaten dinner?" he asked.

"No," she admitted. She had eaten a salad and a roll for lunch at Mr. Hobo's just before the lunchtime rush had started but that had been many hours ago.

"Are you hungry?"

"Yes," she said. "You could even say that I'm starving."

"I am too," Terry said. "And I know just the place where we can go. It is a little out of the way, but the food is great."

"Okay," Leedy said. "I'm always interested in trying out new, out of the way restaurants."

Terry led the way through the dark parking lot. "We can take my car," he said, pointing his thumb at an older-model black convertible Corvette.

"Is that yours?" she asked, pleased.

"Yes."

"Can I drive it?"

"No," he said. "At least not on the first date."

"Is this a date?"

"Yes," he said, leading her to the car.

Leedy smiled. "Oh, boy," she giggled, walking around to the passenger side. "I can't wait to ride in this! I love sports cars."

"Me, too," Terry said, opening the door so she could climb in. "This is Susie. She's a 1976 Stingray and I've had her since I graduated from college."

She sank into the soft black leather seats and felt a rush of excitement. She had been driving her old Jeep for as long as Terry had been driving his Corvette and it felt good to climb into a car that didn't double as a military vehicle.

"Can you put down the roof?" she asked, like a child asking for an ice cream cone.

"I think that could be arranged," he said. He unlatched the front of the ragtop roof from the windshield and pushed a button. The roof began to retract and Leedy yelped with joy as the roof came down. He then handed her a grey overcoat he had gotten from the small dark place behind the bucket seats. "Use this as a blanket, just in case it gets cold," he said, his blue eyes twinkling. Terry climbed in behind the steering wheel and smiled at her. He turned the key and revved the engine. Leedy loved the sound it made. "Ready?" he asked over the noise.

"Oh, yes," she said, pulling the coat up under her chin. "How fast can this baby go?"

"Pretty fast," Terry said. He gave her a wicked grin, then peeled out of the parking lot with tires smoking and the engine screaming. From the sound of things, Leedy guessed they had laid a patch of rubber on the pavement beneath them.

He checked the road for traffic and possible police cruisers before he steadily began to increase their speed. Leedy threw her arms into the air and squealed with delight as the car went faster and faster. The acceleration increased until the street lights along the side of the road had begun to look like pickets on a blurry fence.

"You're going to get me arrested," Terry shouted, glancing into the rearview mirror. "Or killed." But he showed no sign of slowing down the car. Leedy made chicken noises, and he pushed the Corvette to go even faster. They drove along the quiet, deserted streets until even Leedy knew they had to slow down.

"I give up!" Terry yelled over the din of the engine. He

took his foot off the accelerator and the Corvette slowed down. Leedy laughed breathlessly. "I've never taken her this fast," he shouted, laughing too. "You're a crazy lady!"

The car slowed to a respectable speed and Leedy leaned against the soft leather seats and closed her eyes. She was enjoying the feel of the bracing wind against her face. "How's Deanna?" she called, loud enough for him to hear her over the wind and the roar of the engine.

"She's fine," Terry said. "And she isn't allowed to drive my car either."

"How's school going for her?"

"Good, but she isn't home much these days. She has a lot of homework and she has a job at the campus bookstore, not to mention a social life that can only be described as clandestine. I barely see her. We still get together every Sunday though . . . although lately I think she'd rather be spending her time with her friends."

"She's a teenager," Leedy reminded him.

"I know. I know," he said. "But she could drop me a line every month of so. Just to let me know how she's doing. Is that too much to ask?"

"Causing worry is what teenagers do," she sighed. "Ah, to be young and carefree again."

Terry raised an eyebrow. "If memory serves, I recall from your loan application, you're only 27."

"I'll be 28 in three months," she said. "And 30 can't be too far behind!"

"Should I slow down the car?" he asked. "I don't want to frighten you, old girl."

"No way," she said. "As a matter of fact, why don't you see if you can take her up to ninety again?" She felt a thrill as Terry punched the gas pedal all the way down to the floor. It was the most thrilling (if not dangerous) car ride she had ever had.

Ten minutes later, he pulled off a side road and into a parking lot. Leedy looked up and saw they were in front of an old wooden building that was surrounded by a haphazard parking area that was teeming with people.

"Is this it?" she asked. She folded the bulky grey overcoat as best she could and hunted in her purse for a brush for her wind-blown hair.

"Yes," Terry said. "Believe it or not. This is it."

The building hardly looked like a restaurant at all. It looked as if it had once been someone's house which, over many years, had been added onto again and again and again. There was a rambling front porch and what appeared to be a complicated system of wooden decks and staircases that wrapped around the sides of the building. The decks and staircases led to balconies that were filled with people seated in small, round tables. Leedy heard laughter and music coming from the balconies. No one seemed to mind the chilly autumn weather.

Terry parked the car and put the roof back up. He then walked around and opened the door for her, taking her hand and helping her from the car. He silently led her to the front of the building. She looked at the sweeping front porch and saw a large crowd of people waiting to get inside. "This is San Gimigiano Mill," he said, leading her past the throng of people and into the front door.

"Hi, Terry," a pretty, auburn-haired hostess said when they walked in. "Table for two?"

"Hi, Trish," he said warmly. "Yes. Do you have anything in the solarium?"

"Of course," she said. Moments later she led them

through a bustling dining room. It was dark, but cozy, and reminded her of the restaurant that she hoped to someday call her own. Leedy knew immediately she would like it there. The hostess led them past the kitchen and into a large room in the back of the building. Italian cuisine again, she surmised from the decor and aromas. Her favorite.

This room was different from the main dining room. The walls were paneled in what had once been a dark knotty pine wood but had long ago been painted a bright and cheerful white. Each wall was lined with large windows. Hand-painted ivy crept up the sides of the windows and sometimes even onto the ceiling. There were fewer tables in this room than in the main dining room and instead of the soft ivory-colored tablecloths, the linens in the back room were brightly colored floral prints on a black background.

"How is this one?" Trish asked, seating them at a nice table next to a window.

"It's fine," Terry said.

"This is lovely," Leedy said after Trish had left. "But I don't understand how we were seated so quickly. Why didn't we have to wait along with the others?"

"My father and the owner were best friends growing up," he explained. My family has been coming here for years. I hate to cut in line, but I have a starving crazy lady with me. Besides, most of those people you saw outside are waiting to get into the lounge upstairs. They have some good bands performing here, from time to time, and they're popular with the college crowd."

A waitress appeared carrying glasses of water. "Hi, Terry," she said, smiling at them. "Would you like to see the wine list? We have a wonderful 1990 Chateau Leoville-

Barton. It's a Bordeaux red wine. If you would prefer a white wine, we also have a lovely 1993 Lucien Crochet Chene Marchand Sancerre."

"The white wine sounds good," Leedy remarked, and Terry ordered a bottle while she examined the menu. Everything looked delicious. Moments later, the waitress brought them a basket of bread which he offered to her. Inside the basket was an assortment of steaming rolls and muffins and she eagerly chose one.

"I didn't realize how hungry I was," she said, buttering a piece of soft, piping hot black bread. She bit into it and Terry watched her with open admiration. A dollop of butter dropped from the bread and onto her chin.

"Excuse me," she said, embarrassed, reaching for her napkin.

Terry unfolded his napkin and leaned closer to her. "You're very pretty when you're ravenous," he said, dabbing at her chin. He gently rubbed the napkin against her cheek, his hand lingering against her skin.

"I'm sorry," she blushed. He was so close to her that Leedy needed to catch her breath. Instead, she looked into his handsome face and found herself instantly drowning in his blue eyes.

"Um . . . ," he murmured, after a long moment. "The . . . er . . . shrimp dishes here are delicious."

"Really?" she asked, her voice catching.

The waitress had returned, carrying the bottle of wine. She poured a small amount in a glass and handed it to Terry. He sniffed it, dramatically, and then took a small sip. "Perfect," he said, giving the waitress a wink. She poured more wine into his glass and then some in Leedy's.

She took their dinner orders and headed back for the kitchen.

"I'm never sure how I'm supposed to behave when they hand me the wine," he confessed. "I've even thought of gargling with it, but . . ."

"No, silly," Leedy said. "You want to smell it first, to make sure the bouquet is pleasing, then take a small sip and aerate it, like this." She took a sip from her glass and demonstrated the technique as he watched in fascination.

"That's revolting," he said, grimacing at her in mock horror.

"Revolting or not," she said. "That's the way it's done."

They talked about the class lecture, but not for long. The subject matter suddenly seemed not nearly as interesting as each other's company. Soon, the waitress arrived carrying a large tray of food. She set a plate of pasta covered with garlic, tomatoes, and gigantic shrimp in front of Leedy, and a plate of artichoke chicken before Terry. "This looks wonderful," he said.

"It is wonderful," the waitress said before she went back to her work.

Leedy was so hungry, it was all she could do to keep herself from wolfing down the delicious food. "This is so good," she moaned. "I would love to ask the chef for the recipe for his tomato sauce."

"I can get it for you," he said. "Of course, I will not tell him that you're going to be his biggest competition some day."

"Maybe in a few months?"

"Or longer."

"I hope my restaurant is as nice as this one."

"It will be," Terry said, digging into his plate of food

with equal gusto. "Mmm," he said and offered her a forkful of chicken. She took a bite and, it too, was delicious. Leedy ate until her belly was full and then ate some more. When the meal was done, they drank coffee and shared a cannoli.

"Thank you for a lovely dinner," she said. "I can't remember the last time I had a meal this wonderful."

"My pleasure," he said. His eyes met hers and, once again, Leedy had the sensation that she was falling. Falling. Falling. Terry's eyes were incredibly blue and he was looking at her with a look of yearning in his eyes. A look that surrounded her . . . engulfed her. As if he were trying to drink her in.

Terry leaned closer to her and softly . . . gently . . . kissed her.

Leedy kissed him too. His lips were warm and delicious and irresistible. His mouth opened slightly against hers and she melted into him, returning the kiss with a passion that surprised her. He lightly cupped his hand under her chin and pulled her closer to him. His tongue probed her mouth and she felt her insides catch fire with a passion she had never felt before. It felt as if she had never been kissed before. She let her hand slide to his trim waist and felt his glorious body so close to hers.

"No," Leedy moaned, suddenly coming to her senses. "We shouldn't . . ."

She pushed herself away. Terry reluctantly eased back into his chair. He looked around the dining room and saw Trish and the waitress were standing in a nearby corner of the room, smiling at them. "I guess you're right," he said, color rising in his cheeks.

Leedy nodded. "We shouldn't," she said again. "I mean . . . you're my teacher. And my loan officer . . . How would this look? People would say I was kissing you to get a good grade or to get my loan approved . . . Not that that would work."

Terry looked at her curiously for a moment. "You wouldn't do that," he said, decisively. "You're not that kind of person."

"No," she said. "Of course not." But she couldn't help but think . . . would she? She wanted her restaurant with every breath in her body . . . had dreamed of it for most of her life. If kissing Terry, a gorgeous and exciting man, helped to secure a loan, would she do it?

She felt her face flush with guilt. She could never become romantically involved with someone to further her career! Especially someone she had grown to respect. Someone she had even grown to care about. She swallowed the lump that had formed in her throat. Her head ached with the sudden realization that she *liked* Terry, maybe even cared for him beyond a mere friendship. It was an insight she didn't want to acknowledge because it made her yearn for him more. But she wanted her restaurant too. She couldn't imagine kissing him to further her chances of securing her loan. That would be despicable. She could never do anything like that!

Could she?

Terry was watching her from across the table. It was all she could do to keep from jumping into his arms, if only to prove something to herself. "We could go somewhere else . . ." he was whispering.

Just then there was a soft ringing of his cell phone coming from the pocket of his jacket.

"You better answer that," she said, trying hopelessly to slow the pounding of her heart.

"I would rather ignore it," he said, but the other diners were looking at them so he answered it anyway. "Hello," he said, with a slightly impatient edge to his voice. And then, just like the night when Leedy was at his house, the phone call seemed to have an almost imperceptible influence over his demeanor. His body stiffened slightly and his voice dropped an octave. "No," he said. "Is this something that can wait until Tuesday? . . . No . . . I would like to help you, but . . ."

It was her again. Krissy. Somehow Leedy knew, but she didn't know how she knew. The person on the other end of the phone was Krissy Montgomery. Terry would never have been so perturbed if the call had been from Deanna, or from a co-worker. Leedy remembered the way Krissy leaned toward him when she spoke, lightly touching his elbow and whispering in his ear.

She also remembered the look on Brian's face during the final months before their breakup. "It wasn't anyone you know," he had told her. "Just an old friend from school. What's with you these days? You've been acting so suspicious lately. It was just a phone call from a friend. Don't you trust me?"

Leedy felt an icy chill come over her that made her shiver. She watched Terry as he spoke quietly into the phone and felt her throat tighten.

"That would be fine," he was saying, glancing up at her and smiling awkwardly. "We'll talk about it on Tuesday . . . I'll see you then. Good-bye."

He hung up the phone and took Leedy's hand into his. "Sorry about that," he said. "I forgot to turn the stupid thing off."

"That's quite all right," she said but, even to her own ears, her voice sounded formal and prim.

"Are you cold?" he asked, gently rubbing her hands. "We better not take the top off on the way back."

Leedy carefully removed her hands from his and gave him a weak smile. "I think I'm just tired," she said. "Maybe we should be getting back now."

He looked at her, a wounded expression on his face. But all she could think about was the phone call he had just received. How many times had Brian received phone calls from friends and co-workers?

"Are you sure you don't want another cup of coffee?" Terry asked. "Or we could go for a drive . . ." He leaned in closer to her, trying to recapture the moment they had before the phone call, but she pulled away.

"No, thanks," she said. "I better not."

"Can I get you two something else?" the waitress offered, carrying the check in a long black leather sheaf. "More coffee?"

"No, nothing," he said. "It was a wonderful dinner."

"Thanks for coming," the waitress said. There was an amused smile on her face and Leedy didn't understand it until she remembered the kiss she and Terry had shared. She looked around the room and saw that a few of the other customers seated nearby were watching them with the same silly grins on their faces too.

Terry smiled, pulled out her chair and offered her his hand. "Thank you for a lovely evening, Ms. Collins," he said, but there was a hesitation in his touch. As if he thought she might suddenly slap him.

"Thank you," Leedy said, taking his hand. They weren't dating, after all, she told herself. He's free to talk on the phone with anyone who calls him. Even Krissy Montgomery. Terry wrapped his fingers around hers and squeezed softly. They both could sense that something between them had changed. He took her by the hand and led the way back to his car.

"I'm sorry if I was out of line," he said, as they walked back to his car. "I shouldn't have kissed you right there in the restaurant. I'm sorry if I embarrassed you."

"You weren't out of line," she said. "At least not any more out of line than I was."

"And that phone call . . ." Terry said, too quickly. "I have a situation at work that's giving me some trouble. It's nothing I can't handle though." He slipped his arm around her waist. Her body stiffened and she gingerly slipped out of his embrace.

"I lost my head for a moment back in the restaurant," Leedy said, trying to keep her voice even. "I shouldn't have kissed you . . . and I will not let it happen again."

Terry stopped and turned to her. "I wouldn't mind if you did let it happen again, Leedy."

She wanted to say more. She wanted to tell him that his kiss was the most wonderful kiss she had ever known. She wanted to tell him that she was insanely jealous of the woman on the other end of the telephone and she couldn't stand it if there was another woman in his life. She wanted to fall into his arms and have him hold her with his strong arms and kiss her and tell her that everything was all right. But the words remained unspoken. Instead, she looked at her shoes in awkward silence.

Terry watched her for a moment, a confused expression on his face. "Okay," he said, finally. "I . . . um . . . understand. I guess. I'll take you back to your car."

He led her through the parking lot in silence. Leedy thanked him politely when he opened the car door for her. The night had turned cold. It was a good thing Terry had already put the top back on the Corvette. It didn't seem possible that just a few hours earlier, they had been riding through the night with the roof down. She remembered how happy she felt. How excited. She reached across the seat and unlocked the door to let him in. "Thanks," he said as he started the engine. They drove away, neither one knowing what to say. It was a much more sullen trip than the ride in.

"It is getting chilly, isn't it?" Leedy asked, trying to make small talk.

"It sure is," he said, his voice puzzled. She looked out the window and pretended to be engrossed with the view. She couldn't bear to look at him. She knew if she looked at him too long, she'd want to kiss him again. Then she remembered the phone call.

When they finally got back to the parking lot where she had parked her car, she got out of the Corvette quickly. "Thank you for a wonderful dinner," she said, climbing out before he could come around and open the door for her.

"Leedy, I'm sorry about the kiss," Terry said, stumbling out of the car behind her. "No!" he said suddenly. "I take that back. I'm not sorry I kissed you. I want to kiss you again . . ."

"There's no need to apologize," she said, her words catching in her throat. "It was just a kiss. It didn't mean anything." She climbed into her car and started the engine before Terry could say another word. She waved good-bye and pulled her Jeep out of the parking lot, all the while wishing he would somehow stop her.

Terry followed behind her until she was almost home. At first, she thought maybe he was going to follow her to her apartment, but he turned off onto the highway before they reached her street. He gave three quick beeps of his horn and waved, as if nothing had changed between them. She watched him through her rearview mirror as he drove away, thinking about the kiss she could still taste on her lips.

Chapter Eleven

"Then what happened?" Brittany asked.

"Nothing," Leedy said.

"Nothing?"

"He took me back to my car and I went home."

"He didn't kiss you again?"

"No. He didn't kiss me again. I guess it was just one of those . . . moments."

"One of what moments?" Brittany asked, looking disappointed. "How come you two didn't smooch a little in the parking lot?"

"Because," Leedy said, too sharply. "I don't smooch in parking lots! And he's my instructor . . . and the loan officer at the bank. Besides, I'm not a sixteen-year-old, you know."

"So what?" Brittany scoffed. "You don't have to be a teenager to enjoy a good old-fashioned smooching in a parking lot. In fact, don't knock it until you've tried it!

And, may I remind you, there is only two more weeks left of your night class."

Leedy was beginning to regret that she had told Brittany about the kiss she and Terry had shared. "Brit, he got another phone call," Leedy reminded her. "And I'm sure it was a woman."

"So what?" she said. "That call could have been about anything."

"It could have been," Leedy said. "But it wasn't. I could tell by the way he was speaking into the phone. I think it might have been Krissy Montgomery . . ."

"Is that the bimbo you told me about? The one who keeps giving you dirty looks? From class?" Brittany asked, dismissing the notion with a sweep of her hand. "Jo Anne already told you he wasn't interested in her. Besides, if you're so concerned that he might be seeing someone, why don't you ask him?"

The question left Leedy speechless. Ask him? Well, of course, that did seem like the logical, not to mention obvious, thing to do. And leave it to Brittany to point out the most adult course of action. But . . .

"I don't know," Leedy said at last. "It doesn't feel like a question I can ask him yet. Right now, it feels like smooching with the loan officer in the parking lot is . . . wrong."

Brittany's mouth dropped open. "Leedy!" she exclaimed. "Your loan was declined, remember? And I was not suggesting you smooch with the loan officer in an effort to push through the paperwork. I was only suggesting that you act on feelings that you and I both know you have. Feelings that are healthy and natural and good!"

"I know," Leedy said. "You're right, Brit. But . . . But . . . It's just that I don't know where I stand with him and I need to concentrate on my career . . . Can we talk about this later? Or better still, not at all? We should get back to work."

Brittany shrugged. "Fine," she said and headed for the kitchen.

Leedy pretended to check the coffee stations. By the time she had restocked the already full cabinet with supplies, she felt ashamed of herself. She remembered the delighted expression on Brittany's face when she told her about Terry's kiss in the restaurant. Brittany was happy Leedy had found a romance.

"I'm sorry," Leedy said, when she found Brittany headed for the dish room with a tray full of dirty coffee cups. "It's just that . . . It's like this . . ."

Brittany waited, her chin sticking out stubbornly. "It's like what?"

"I don't know," Leedy said, searching for the words. "This was the second time Terry got a phone call. And you should see the way she looks at him in class. It's as if she wants to peel her clothes off and climb on top of him! The whole thing reminds me of the way it was before Brian and I broke up. The hushed voices over the phone and the darting eyes. I know Terry isn't my boyfriend and he's free to see anyone he . . ."

"Brian?" Brittany said, cocking her head to the side. "Is that why you're so worked up over this? Oh, Leedy . . . Brian is ancient history. Besides, it was a different situation altogether. You had been together with Brian for a few years and he didn't even have the decency to tell you the truth about Angela! I know it was a painful experience, but not all men are like him."

"I know," Leedy said. "But it's hard to believe Terry has no one in his life. You've seen him, Brit. He's a handsome man and . . ."

"And from everything I've heard about him, he's a *nice* man," Brittany said. "And he's also a man who obviously likes you too. Don't you see that?"

She shrugged. "No," she said. "I don't see it."

"Well, you should," Brittany said. "Everyone else does. Oh, by the way, and I'm speaking for women everywhere when I say this, you can have a career *and* a romance at the same time."

"Really?"

"Yes," Brittany sighed. "People do it every day. Mark and I are both full-time students, remember? We juggle classes, jobs, family, and a so-called social life and we have a romance. As a matter of fact, we wouldn't have it any other way."

"I know it can be done," Leedy said. "But . . ."

"But what?"

"But . . . Terry hasn't asked me for a date. Not a real date anyway. Just impromptu after-class get-togethers. Usually with Jo Anne."

Brittany considered this carefully and then shrugged. "Weren't you the one who made it clear that you didn't want to see him while you're still a student in his class?"

Leedy shrugged. "Well . . . yes. But . . ."

"He's only respecting your wishes. But the sparks are flying, aren't they?"

"Yes."

"Then why don't you tell him you've changed your mind? Why don't you ask him out on a date?"

"I could never do that," Leedy protested.

"Yes you can," Brittany said. "As a matter of fact, as I recall, your RSVP to my wedding said you were bringing along a guest . . ."

Leedy blinked. When she had responded to Brittany's invitation a month ago, she had assumed she could find someone to escort her to the wedding. She had even considered calling up her cousin Frank. But now . . .

"Why don't you invite Terry to my wedding?" Brittany asked. "The date falls the week after your class ends. It will be fun."

"Yes, but . . ."

"You have a class tonight, don't you?"

"Yes. I do, but . . ." Leedy's face suddenly went pale and she looked at her watch. "Oh, dear," she said. "I better hurry or I'm going to be late for that class!"

Leedy gave Brittany a sudden, hard hug and then headed to the employees' locker room. She quickly changed into her faded blue jeans and an old argyle sweater. She thought of Krissy Montgomery and wondered what she was going to wear to class tonight. Probably a sequined ball gown. Leedy suddenly wished she had brought something nicer to wear to class, but it was too late. She grabbed her bookbag and rushed back to the dining room.

"Wish me luck!" she called to Brittany as she hurried past.

"Good luck!" Brittany said, slapping her a high-five.

Leedy gave her a thumbs-up and bounded out the door. She was late and traffic made her even later. Class had already begun by the time she pulled into the parking lot.

"Sorry I'm late," Leedy whispered to Terry when she finally made her way into class a few minutes later. Krissy Montgomery rolled her eyes and smiled at Terry. He ignored her and went back to his lecture. Leedy found her seat and took out her notebook and pen. She then pulled out the tape recorder and hit the RECORD button.

Jo Anne grinned at her. "Hey girl," she whispered.

Leedy watched Terry and tried to concentrate on what he was saying. He looked handsome in his khaki slacks and a dark blue, long-sleeved polo shirt. Leedy was thankful she had finally bought the tape recorder. Now she had an excuse to watch her instructor for the entire class. And watching Terry was all she wanted to do. Now and then, she noticed him look her way. When this happened, her heart would race and she'd look at him shyly. He would smile at her with an expression of curious reserve on his face. Then he'd go on with his lecture.

"Would you and Terry like to go out for coffee after class?" she asked Jo Anne. She was thinking about what Brittany had said, but she knew she'd never have the nerve to ask him to the wedding, especially with Jo Anne there. But it was the only excuse she could think of to see him.

"Sorry, Leedy," Jo Anne said. "Riley was sick today and I want to relieve Ted on nurse detail. You and Terry go on without me."

Leedy wished for that very thing, but it was not to be. She had rehearsed the invitation over and over in her heard. "Coffee?" she would ask, as if it didn't matter one way or the other if he went with her or not. Or maybe she should try the more direct approach and say, "Can we get together after class? I'd like to talk to you about a personal matter."

Terry was speaking, but she barely heard what he said.

"That's it for tonight, folks. We'll meet again on Tuesday." Leedy started packing up her bags quickly, hurrying to beat Krissy to the punch, but she was too late. Krissy was already standing next to him, tossing her long, silky hair and hanging onto every word he said.

"I'll walk with you to your car," a dejected Leedy told Jo Anne.

"Sure," she said. "Let's wait for Terry."

Jo Anne and Leedy made their way slowly to the front of the room, both hoping the harem would exit soon.

"Hi," he said when they walked up. He was watching Leedy, his expression hesitant, but hopeful. Krissy Montgomery turned, gave them a cool stare and then turned back to Terry.

"Are you ready?" she chirped, once more tossing her glorious blonde hair.

Terry's eyes darted to Leedy. "I'm just taking Krissy to . . ." he began, but Krissy was pulling on his arm.

"Let's not be late," she cooed, tugging on the waist of his shirt.

"I'll walk you ladies to your car," he said, ignoring her.

Leedy felt uncomfortable, following behind Terry and Krissy as they walked to the parking lot. Jo Anne walked next to her, but Leedy still felt as if she was intruding on Terry and Krissy's private party.

"Here you go, Mrs. Cleaver," Krissy snipped to Jo Anne under her breath.

"Why, thank you, dearie," Jo Anne said biting out the words. She looked over at Terry, but realized he hadn't heard her snide remark. He was too busy studying Leedy's stiff, frozen expression.

"I'll . . . um . . . see you soon," he said slowly when

Leedy turned toward her Jeep. Was it her imagination, or did he have something more to say?

"Ta ta," Krissy said, taking Terry by the arm and pulling him toward the Corvette. "Don't wait up for us."

Leedy tried to think of something clever to say, but all she managed was; "See you in class next week." She could almost hear Brittany groan, but it was no use. Clearly, Terry's attention was directed elsewhere and this was not the time or the place to talk. His attention was directed at Krissy. Leedy started her engine and tried not to watch as the two walked to his Corvette. Terry was speaking to her, his face serious, but she couldn't hear what he was saying.

Leedy looked the other way and didn't look at them again until she drove past on her way out of the parking lot. Krissy was sitting in the passenger seat of Terry's car, leaning toward him seductively. He was behind the steering wheel. He glanced up at Leedy and waved as she drove past him at full tilt. She looked away quickly, but not before she saw that Krissy was leaning toward him, practically sitting on his lap, with her full, firm breasts pressing against him. Leedy fixed her eyes on the exit of the parking lot. She forced herself not to look in the rearview mirror because she knew he had still not started his car.

"I'm going to open up my own restaurant someday," Leedy said out loud as she drove onto the main road. "And it's going to be the best restaurant in town." But somehow the sentence, one she had said to herself thousands and thousands of times, didn't feel quite the same this time. She still wanted her own restaurant, but she wanted Terry Foster even more.

Chapter Twelve

It was only early November, but the shops in the mall were already trimmed for Christmas. Green and red decorations adorned every window from the card shop to the pet store to the food court. Wreaths made of plastic lined the walls, and motion-sensitive Santas began to sing or chuckle merrily whenever anyone got too close.

"Can't we get through with Halloween before the Christmas season begins?" Deanna grumbled. "At least let us celebrate Thanksgiving. That's still three weeks away! I wish we could enjoy one holiday at a time, don't you, Leedy?"

"I agree with you one hundred percent," Leedy said. It had been less than a week since she had spent that time with Terry, but it felt more like years. The scheduled shopping trip with Deanna had made her restless since Sunday. Maybe Deanna could provide more information about her uncle's mysterious phone calls. Not that Leedy could bring herself to grill Deanna about Terry's comings and goings. That was, after all, his own personal business.

Deanna was wearing her long blond hair in two braids, like a teenage Rebecca of Sunnybrook Farm, and sipping on a caramel frappuccino. They had already taken the burdensome bookbag to Leedy's car for safekeeping and had returned to the coffee shop so they could sit down and formulate a plan of attack for their shopping activities.

"I want to go to that shoe store again," Deanna said. "I have to take back the running shoes. I got them home and they like, I don't know, felt funny. Thank goodness I never took them out for a run."

Leedy nodded. It was all she could do to keep her mind on the conversation at hand when all she wanted to do was ask for news about Terry. "Have you been running much?" she fished.

"Nah. I've got too much homework to do to be able to run."

"Oh. How about your uncle? Has he been able to get out and run?" As soon as the words came out of her mouth, she regretted saying them. Surely Deanna could see through her thinly disguised efforts to pump her for information.

"I think he runs at lunch sometimes," she said, with a shrug. "There's a gym in his office building with a treadmill. Maybe he gets a few miles in on that."

"Oh," Leedy said, thoughtfully. "Do you want to check at the sports store for another pair of running shoes?" She was pleased with herself because she had managed to ask a question that didn't involve Terry.

"That's a good idea," Deanna said, and they took to the mall. Leedy promised herself she wouldn't mention Terry's name again. Even if she was dying. But, on the other hand, if Deanna should happen to bring up the subject of her uncle, she wouldn't stop her.

No, Leedy told herself. *You're not to bother Deanna with your childish games. If you want to find out if Terry is seeing Krissy Montgomery, then you just have to ask him yourself. Don't drag Deanna into this!* Then she sighed. Of course he was seeing her. Hadn't Leedy seen with her own two eyes how Krissy had practically given him a lap dance in his car!

"Your uncle told me he was having some sort of problem at work," Leedy asked, all reservations thrown out the window. "Is everything all right?"

"I don't know," Deanna said with a shrug. "He had some kind of date on Saturday night and I went to the football game on Sunday. I have not seen Uncle Terry since Saturday"

A date! Leedy's heart sank. "Oh," she mumbled.

"You'll see him when you drop me off at home," Deanna said. "Maybe we can have Chinese food again."

After that Leedy couldn't think of much more to talk about with Deanna. She asked her about school and her studies, but something seemed to be lacking from their conversation. So preoccupied with Terry, she didn't feel the usual spark of enthusiasm she always felt when Deanna was around.

Leedy sighed and tried on another pair of shoes. "I don't know," she said to Deanna. "I couldn't wear these to work, that's for certain. Not and be able to walk properly. What do you think?"

"I love impractical shoes," Deanna said, a giggle in her voice. "There's nothing like the feeling of pinched toes and an aching instep to make a girl feel pretty. That's what I always say."

Leedy smiled. It was no use. She had to find out the truth about Terry. "I have an idea," she said. "Let's go to the Nail Jail and get a manicure . . . and a pedicure. My treat." Deanna's eyes lit up. Surely there was nothing wrong with two friends having a juicy gossip session while they were having their nails done.

A few minutes later, Deanna and Leedy were seated next to each other in the pedicure chairs, bottles of Mocha Frost Kiss and Autumn Burgundy Creme waiting for them nearby. Leedy closed her eyes, waiting for the right moment, and enjoyed the gentle but firm massage provided by the woman in the pink smock.

"This is heavenly," Deanna sighed. "I've never had my feet massaged before."

"I have only done this once myself," Leedy admitted. "But I think I'm going to start to make a habit of it."

"Yeah," Deanna chirped. "We could do this once a month together."

Leedy's mood lifted at the thought of their shopping trips becoming a regular occurrence. Even if Terry had found someone else, there was no reason why she couldn't remain friends with Deanna.

"Tell me about Chris," Leedy asked, trying to take her mind off her thoughts.

"Are you sure you want to hear this?" Deanna asked. Her face flushed at the sound of her boyfriend's name. "I better warn you. I get all goofy when I talk about him. My friends say it's so gaggy . . . But I can't seem to help myself."

"I want to hear every detail," Leedy said, sliding back into the seat.

"I met him in my English 101 class," she began. "He asked to borrow a pencil. I thought he was pretty much of a bone head not to have a pencil on the first day of class, but I gave him one anyway. And just as I gave him the pencil, he dropped his bookbag and a case full of pens and pencils dropped to the floor."

Leedy smiled. "I think he wanted to meet you."

Deanna smiled back and nodded. "Ah, yeah! You think? He kind of started talking to me after that. Just the usual questions. He asked me about my major and my roommate in the dorm. Was she a geek or cool? Where was I from? All the normal stuff you talk about. But it was as if he was hanging onto my every word. I've never had a guy so interested in my life . . . except for Uncle Terry, of course. Chris waited a couple of days and then he asked me to go to a movie."

"He sounds great," Leedy said. "What movie did you see?"

"To tell you the truth, I don't even remember. All I know is that he held my hand and we went to get a slice of pizza afterwards. It was the best pizza I've ever eaten!"

Leedy smiled. It was a cute story of young romance, but Deanna told it in such a way that it seemed to take on the feel of an epic love story.

"I'm a little taller than he is," she said, her face clouding with worry. "But just by an inch or two. And he's still growing. Uncle Terry once told me it takes boys longer to finish growing. He says I won't always be taller than all the boys. He says they'll catch up."

"I've heard that too," Leedy said. "And even if Chris doesn't grow any taller, so what?"

"Yeah. I know. I know. I like being tall most of the time, but it scares some guys away."

"I understand how you feel," Leedy said. "I'm five foot nine. It doesn't sound as if it bothers Chris though."

"No," Deanna said. "Not in the least."

"Does it bother you?"

"Sometimes," she admitted. "But not always."

"If it doesn't bother you and it doesn't bother him, then it doesn't matter who's an inch or two taller. Does it?"

Deanna nodded and sank back into the pedicure chair, shutting her eyes wearily. "I don't care about the height thing," she yawned. "Chris is there on tennis scholarship."

"Oh, he's an athlete? That's good."

"Yes, but he isn't into it as much as he used to be. He enjoys it, but he doesn't think he can make a career of it. He's studying to be a mechanical engineer, with a minor in astronomy. He's teaching me about the constellations and the planets. I know it sounds silly, but it is really interesting."

"Watching the stars sounds romantic," Leedy said.

"It is romantic," Deanna sighed. "But that isn't all we do. We both enjoy bike riding and we go to all the football games. We have a lot of fun together!"

"He sounds great," Leedy said.

"I finally told Uncle Terry about him," Deanna admitted.

The sound of Terry's name made Leedy's heart skip a beat. "Really?" she said.

"I thought he'd be mad at me for getting all goo-goo eyed," Deanna said, her voice rising in excitement. "But he said he had a feeling I was dating someone. He said he knew I was a level-headed young woman and would make good decisions." She was beaming.

"That's good," Leedy said. "See, you didn't have anything to worry about after all."

"I guess I didn't," Deanna said. "Uncle Terry says he wants to meet Chris, but that's so lame! I can't take him home to meet my family yet! Chris would think I'd gone goofy on him."

Leedy only halfway listened while Deanna chattered excitedly about her new-found romance. It wasn't that she was disinterested in her young friend's life, it was just that her thoughts were far away. She remembered Terry in the restaurant parking lot with the expression of longing and confusion on his handsome face. Things had gone so well between them that night. What had happened? Of course, Leedy knew the answer had been the telephone call. One stupid, little phone call had kicked her dreams right in the teeth, almost as certainly as the bank's loan approval committee had done only a few short weeks ago.

"Is your uncle seeing someone?" Leedy asked suddenly.

Deanna's eyes popped open wide and she looked at Leedy with surprise. "No," she said. "At least, I don't think so. I don't see him all week and we keep our weekends open for each other. He had a date on Saturday. I think. But it may have had something to do with work. He didn't seem too excited. Uncle Terry would tell me if there were someone serious in his life, and he hasn't mentioned anyone." Leedy felt a rush of relief. And disappointment. Terry had not told Deanna about another woman. But he had not mentioned her either.

"Why do you ask?" Deanna asked, her face full of interest.

Leedy blinked a few times, not wanting to make a full confession. "I don't know," she stammered. "I was just curious. You had mentioned his date on Saturday. I was just wondering if it was anyone I know . . ."

Leedy hoped Deanna would volunteer some more information, but she didn't. "I went to a party on campus," she said. "He didn't tell me anything about it but he was home by the time I got home that night. But, like I said, it may have been a business meeting and not a real date."

Deanna was watching Leedy intently, her face was bright, her eyebrows raised. She waited for Leedy to explain her questions regarding her uncle's love life, but it soon became clear that nothing more was forthcoming. Finally she spoke. "Are you interested in Uncle Terry?" Leedy blushed, then shrugged. "Come on," Deanna prodded. "Fess up! I told you about Chris."

"There's nothing to confess to," Leedy said. The manicurist was painting her toenails and the color looked too dark. But Deanna was looking at her, clearly skeptical of the denial. "Oh, all right," Leedy said. "I'll tell you, but it's got to stay between the two of us. Deal?"

"Deal."

"I didn't like your uncle at first." Leedy admitted with an embarrassed smile. "It wasn't his fault though. The bank rejected my loan application and I just about burst into tears during the meeting. I think I made a fool out of myself."

"He told me about that," Deanna said. "He didn't mention your name, of course, but he told me the whole story. He came home from work and told me he'd made a beautiful woman cry in his office that day. I didn't realize it was you."

"He said that?" Leedy exclaimed, her face turning pink.

"Yes. He also said he was thinking about calling you but he said you were so sad when you left the bank you would probably just hang up on him."

Leedy gulped, taken aback by this startling new information. "He really said that?" she stammered. "I never knew! I wonder why he never called."

"I don't know," Deanna said. "I guess because you were embarrassed. But, if it means anything to you, it was his idea to go to Mr. Hobo's for dinner that first night I met you. And he gave me ten bucks for finding out that you were going to be running in the race the next day . . ."

"He did that?" These revelations were almost too much to take in.

"He gave me ten dollars!" Deanna said again. "He told me I was a good detective and he should bring me with him all the time. I guess that was when you signed up for his class." While she talked Leedy nodded to her every word. Her heart was pounding with happiness and her mind was racing with things she wanted to tell Terry when she saw him. After she covered his face with soft, tender butterfly kisses.

"He really said all those things?"

"Yes," Deanna said. "But don't tell him I told you. I'm usually really good about not telling my uncle's business, but this time I think it's best that I butt in."

That was enough for Leedy. She could hardly wait for the manicurist to finish painting her toenails. When they finally left the Nail Jail, Leedy practically dragged Deanna through the mall to finish the rest of their shopping. Every few moments, she'd look at her watch. The day went by slowly until it was finally time to go.

"Do you have anything else you need?" she asked, trying to hide her restlessness.

"This should do it for the week," Deanna said, holding up two shopping bags.

"Great!" Leedy said, and pointed Deanna toward her car. Of course, they had to make a few unplanned stops along the way out of the mall, but Leedy happily acquiesced to anything the teenager wanted to do.

Leedy had to control herself to keep from speeding as she drove Deanna home. She couldn't wait to see Terry. Couldn't wait to get him outside on the patio where she could finally, at long last, tell him the way she felt about him. She would tell him that she liked him. Really, *really* liked him. It sounded sophomoric, but they were words that had to, at long last, be spoken. And if he should happen to kiss her again, that would be perfectly fine with her.

She turned the corner onto Terry's street, slowing down only slightly as she rounded the curve. She could see his house from a block away. She could see the black Corvette in the driveway. He was home! But wait, there was another car there too. A bright red BMW sports car squatted in the driveway next to Terry's Corvette. It looked, to her at least, decidedly out of place in front of his house.

Just then the front door opened, and she saw two figures standing in the doorway. They paused a moment, as if in deep conversation. Leedy carefully coasted her Jeep up to the curb and slowed to a stop.

"Aren't you coming in?" Deanna asked as she gathered her bookbag and packages. "I thought we were having Chinese food with Uncle Terry?"

"I don't know," Leedy said, glancing at the shadows in the doorway. "Maybe I shouldn't. It looks like you have company. Come to think of it, I should go in to work tonight. The new assistant chef is there by himself. The regular chef has the night off." It was a lie, but one she couldn't help making. She tried not to look at the entrance of the house. If she could just let Deanna out of the car before anyone saw her, maybe she could get away without interrupting Terry and his . . . guest.

He was standing in the doorway to the house. He had not noticed when Leedy pulled up. He was talking intently to a woman who was facing him, her back to the street. That back looked uncomfortably familiar. It was a woman's back. A woman who wore a pair of tight designer blue jeans and a long pumpkin-colored sweater coat that looked as if it cost the proverbial pretty penny. She had long, perfectly coifed blond hair. Leedy's mouth dropped open when she realized the woman was no other than Krissy Montgomery.

Deanna looked at Leedy's shocked face and then at the doorway to the house. "It isn't what you think, Leedy," she whispered. "That woman is one of Uncle Terry's students. She drops by sometimes for help with . . ."

"It's okay," Leedy said, pasting a smile on her face. "Your uncle has no ties to me. And I know Krissy. She's in the class. She's a lovely person." It was all she could do to choke the words out, but somehow she managed to keep her face frozen in a tense smile.

To her horror, she realized that Terry and Krissy were watching them as Deanna climbed out of her car. Leedy smiled and waved, all the while pretending her heart had not just been broken.

Krissy slid her arm around Terry's waist and pulled him to her, smiling at Leedy with perfect pink lips. "Hi y'all!"

she chimed, leaning in and whispering something in his ear. There was a victorious expression on her face that made Leedy think of words she never said in mixed company. But, somehow, she managed to keep smiling.

"Leedy, wait!" Terry called, pulling away from Krissy's tight grip.

"I can't," Leedy shouted through the open car door. "I have to get to work! Thanks for the shopping trip, Deanna."

"Same time next week?" the girl asked, holding onto the car door.

"Sure thing," Leedy said. She realized she was smiling like a lunatic, but she didn't dare stop grinning. Deanna hesitated, but finally shut the car door. Leedy waved one last time before she stomped down hard on the gas pedal. She didn't mean for it to happen, but the tires on her Jeep squealed angrily as she drove away from the house.

She looked into the rearview mirror and saw Krissy and Deanna standing in the front yard, watching the Jeep as it laid a patch of rubber. Terry was there too, but he was standing on the sidewalk, waving for Leedy to come back.

Chapter Thirteen

It was the last night of class. Leedy's weekend had gone by in a blur of work and wishing the phone would ring. When it did ring, she refused to answer it. When she returned home late at night and saw that the little red light of her answering machine was flashing, she refused to listen to her messages. It had been the longest four days of her life. She had considered skipping the last class but somehow the suggestion made her angry. Why should she not get her money's worth out of a class that had proven itself to be beneficial to her career? Why should she let a tryst between Krissy Montgomery and Terry Foster deter her from receiving a quality education?

Terry called. Repeatedly. She knew because she was there when the calls came in. He left messages on her machine, asking her to call him. But Leedy decided not to. She wasn't ready to talk to him. Not then, anyway. She was afraid of what he would say.

She worked a double shift every day until Monday afternoon when Brittany had angrily ordered her out of Mr. Hobo's. Once, she spotted Terry sitting by himself in the dining room. Leedy hid out in the kitchen while Brittany told him she wasn't there.

But it was now Tuesday and her resolve was all gone. She missed him terribly and it was the last day of class. Leedy greeted the day with mixed emotions. She knew she had to face him sooner or later, but the thought of seeing him again made her feel queasy. She couldn't get the image of Krissy standing in Terry's doorway, gently tugging on his arm, out of her mind. None of that mattered any more, Leedy told herself. The day of the last class had finally come and she had no intention of missing it, Krissy Montgomery or not.

She sat at her desk and grimly opened her notebook, flipping through the pages and pages of notes she had taken over the past six weeks. She had played her tape recordings of the lectures over and over again, as much to hear the sound of Terry's voice as to pretend to study. Leedy sighed. She wished she had taken the class before she had applied for the bank loan. These notes would have come in handy back then. And maybe, with a different beginning for them, her first meeting with him might have gone better. Maybe things would have been different now.

Terry walked into the classroom, a determined swing to his walk. He gently pushed past the gaggle of students in the front of the room. He was looking for her, Leedy realized when she saw his eyes go straight to her desk. When he saw her, his face filled with relief. "Leedy," he called, but the students were already closing in on him, slapping him on the back and making jokes. Included in the crowd was Miss Perfect Blond, herself. This time she was wearing a pair of red hip-hugging denim bell-bottom pants and a clingy black knit sweater.

Leedy grimaced and dug in her bag for her pencil case, pretending she hadn't seen him. But she couldn't help but watch him as he stood in the front of the room while Krissy fawned over him. Was it her imagination or were Krissy's outfits getting tighter and more daring with each class? He was nodding at Krissy, but his eyes were on Leedy. He was listening to something she was saying, all the while nodding impatiently. Leedy wished Krissy was not leaning so close to him, and wished even more that she was not blocking his path to her desk.

Terry looked fleetingly across the room at her. Suddenly, he took Krissy's hand off his arm and whispered something to her. His face stern and resolute as he pressed past her. "Leedy," he called when he saw she was watching him. She quickly looked away. She started to count to one hundred, but only made it to seven before she looked back up again. He was standing in front of her desk, looking down at her. There was a look in his eye, as if they were the only two people in the room. His expression was hopeful and determined. His eyes met hers and he smiled. She returned the gaze, almost hesitantly, and found herself returning the smile. One look at him and her difficult weekend was all but forgotten and she was melting under his gaze.

"I need to see you after class," he said firmly, not caring about the women in the front of the classroom who were watching him.

"I don't know . . . I . . ." she stammered.

"Yes," he said, almost commanding her. "Please . . . We need to talk."

"All right," she agreed, helpless to refuse him.

He smiled, his face awash with relief. "I can't wait," he said, quietly, so that only she could hear him. Then he returned to the front of the room and stood in front of the class. Again, his eyes found hers, as if he couldn't look away.

"Okay, everyone," he said finally, when he realized the class was waiting. "Please, sit down. We need to begin." Krissy reluctantly took her seat, but she was watching him as intently as he was watching Leedy.

"I know this is our last day of class," he said. "But we still have a lot of ground to cover. So, let's get started."

Just then, Jo Anne darted into the room, mumbling apologies to Terry. Leedy smiled at her as she dropped her books on her desk. "Late, as usual," she whispered, her cheeks a bright shade of pink. "Ryan's football practice ran longer than I expected." She brushed a loose curl out of her eyes and leaned over toward Leedy. "Can we get together for coffee after class?" she asked. "I have an important business proposition I would like to discuss with you."

"Um . . . well. Terry said he needed to speak with me after class," Leedy whispered.

"He's coming too," Jo Anne said. "I called him this morning. He said he would tell you. I would have called you earlier, but you haven't been answering the phone lately. I left you three messages yesterday. Is your machine on the fritz?"

"Yes," Leedy lied. Had Jo Anne called? She couldn't remember. The only thing she remembered was Terry's voice when she finally played his messages, over and over again.

Her heart sank. Maybe Terry didn't want to talk to her

at all. Maybe he was just passing on the message that Jo Anne wanted to meet for coffee after class. But his face had been so earnest, his whisper so insistent. "I can't wait," he had said. What did that mean?

The rest of the class passed quickly and Leedy barely heard a word Terry said. She was too busy watching his expressive and handsome face and wondering what it would be like to feel his strong arms around her and taste his mouth on hers. Twice she caught him look in her direction. Both times, when he saw she was watching him, he looked as if he wanted to call out to her. And there was that expression again, if only for an almost imperceptible second. She did sense that he was attracted to her, she admitted—or maybe it was only wishful thinking on her part. Or maybe he was a player who juggled women for fun. But that didn't seem right either.

"Are you ready?" Jo Anne asked.

"Huh?" she said, lost in her troubled thoughts.

"Earth to Leedy," Jo Anne said, laughing. "Class is over, sweetie. We can go now."

"Oh . . . I'm sorry," Leedy said, embarrassed. It didn't seem possible two hours had gone by so quickly—and so tortuously slow, all at the same time.

She gathered up her things. The problem, she decided, was that she didn't know where she stood with Terry. And she didn't know where he stood with Krissy Montgomery. "It's about time I found out," she told herself as she stuffed her books into her bag. "Once and for all."

"Did you say something?" Jo Anne asked.

"Oh . . . um . . . no," Leedy shrugged, nodding in the direction of Terry's desk. "He seems to be busy. I just wonder if we should meet him there."

"Terry might need a minute to escape his fan club," Jo Anne said in agreement. "But we can wait."

Leedy reminded herself, for the hundredth time, that Terry was single . . . and gorgeous . . . and those women were only human. So am I, she wanted to shout out loud. So am I!

Krissy was standing next to Terry, her hand, once again, was lightly touching his elbow. She looked in Leedy's direction and saw that she was watching. Krissy pursed her lips into a sneer and slipped her hand onto his back.

"That Krissy," Jo Anne said indignantly, shaking her head. "Could she be more of a floozy? I'm surprised she had the nerve to even show her face here tonight after what she did last week!"

"What do you mean?" Leedy asked, confused.

"Didn't you hear?" Jo Anne asked. "You gotta start checking the messages on your answering machine more often, sweetie. I told you. I've been trying to call you for days!"

"I worked double shifts all weekend," Leedy apologized. "What happened?"

"Well, you know how Krissy has been throwing herself at Terry since the first day of class?" Jo Anne said, her voice low and her eyes darting toward the front of the room.

"I suppose," Leedy said. "But Terry's a big boy. He can take care of himself."

"True," Jo Anne said. "But I don't think you know the whole story. But take my word for it, Miss Diplomat, Krissy Montgomery hasn't been exactly forthright in her ongoing efforts to . . . become better acquainted with our class instructor. It's been the talk of the coffee machine.

I'm surprised you didn't know. Ever since the first day of class, she has been requesting extra help with her 'homework,' if you know what I mean. She wanted to talk with him about accounting or banking or whatever after class, at her place, of course."

"Well," Leedy asked, sticking her chin out. "Terry is a bachelor and a red-blooded, healthy young man, and Krissy is an attractive young . . . woman. They're both consenting adults, Jo Anne. They can do whatever they want."

Jo Anne snorted. "Oh, Krissy's pretty enough, I suppose. If you like the high-dollar tramp look. And she certainly makes the most of her assets. But it's not her looks that are the problem."

"I don't understand."

Jo Anne leaned in, almost whispering in Leedy's ear. "Krissy cornered Terry one day and told him she wanted a list of his clients."

"Why would Krissy want that?" Leedy asked, confused. Jo Anne looked at Leedy's blank expression and sighed.

"You're such a sweet little apple dumpling, aren't you?" Jo Anne said, shaking her head. "You have no idea how the Krissy Montgomerys of the world do business, do you?"

"I'm sorry, Jo Anne," Leedy said. "But I don't have any idea what you're talking about."

"I will spell it out for you then," Jo Anne said. "Krissy asked Terry for a list of his clients, along with a favorable letter of reference."

"That's a bit forward of her," Leedy admitted.

"That's not all," Jo Anne said. She glanced up at the front of the room again and saw that the flock of students vying for Terry's attention was thinning out. "Krissy told him she was willing to do 'almost anything' to get a favorable recommendation from Madison's favorite banker." Jo Anne added the word 'almost' reluctantly.

"Recommendation for what?"

"Krissy wants to be the financial planner for all the movers and shakers in town. Of course, no one in their right mind would turn their investments over to her, after that sticky business with the very rich and very old Mr. Hancock. Naturally, Terry saw through her right away. He's no fool. He thought he was safe after the first time she finished his class, but she just enrolled in the class again. And again. So far, he's managed to keep his distance from her. At least, up until last week."

"What *happened* last week?" Leedy asked. Her breathing had become irregular and her heart was pounding. Every fiber of her existence suddenly depended on the next words that would come out of Jo Anne's mouth.

"Krissy called him. She asked if he wouldn't mind giving her a lift to pick up her car at the garage after class. She said it would only take ten minutes . . . she said it was at that place on Fitzpatrick?" Leedy nodded in understanding. "Krissy said she had her brakes replaced and she had no way to pick up her car."

"Okay," Leedy shrugged. "So her car was in the shop."

"And maybe pigs can fly!" Jo Anne exclaimed, putting her hands on her hips. A few people in front of the room turned and glanced at them. "Anyway," Jo Anne continued, her voice dropping to a whisper. "Terry saw no harm in doing Krissy this one favor. But once he had her in his car, she was all over him! She told him she had fallen madly in love with him and wanted to spend the rest of her life proving it. She all but tore his clothes off—right there in the parking lot!"

Leedy flinched, remembering seeing Terry and Krissy sitting in his car. She remembered how he seemed to want to say more. "How do you know all this?" Leedy blurted, her eyes darting to the front of the room. Terry was standing, with his back toward them, firmly reclaiming his elbow from Krissy's determined grip.

"My husband told me all about it," Jo Anne whispered. "Terry and Ted have lunch together a few times a month, remember? Of course, Ted thought the whole thing was hysterically funny. He said Terry told him Krissy admitted her car was safe and sound at home. She said it was the only way she could think of to finally get him alone!"

Leedy tried to imagine Terry alone in a dark parking lot with a beautiful, willing woman, but the image was too painful. "What did he do?" she asked, her voice breaking.

"I would have pushed her out onto the street and driven away! But you know Terry. He's too much of a gentleman for his own good. Ted said Terry drove Krissy to her house but then it took him nearly another hour to finally get her out of his car! Ted thought it was pretty darn amusing that Terry would be in such a soup. He said he wished he had to fight off beautiful women that way. But, as you may have already guessed, my husband is an idiot."

Leedy was stunned. She looked at the front of the classroom. All the other students had finally filed out of the room except for Krissy. She was talking to Terry, or, judging by the body language, arguing with him. Her hands were in tight little fists that were perched on her hips defiantly. She was shaking her head, her face an expression of tight control, her eyes glaring at him angrily. Terry was speaking to her, his rugged jaw clenched and his face determined. Leedy wished she could hear what he was saying.

"That's not all!" Jo Anne continued, her eyes flashing in anger. "Ted said he called Terry yesterday just to rib him about this whole Krissy situation and found out that she had the nerve to show up at his *house*! Right there in front of Deanna and everything!"

"I know," Leedy said. "I was dropping Deanna off from the mall and saw them together, standing in the doorway."

"What did you do?" Jo Anne gasped. "Boy, I wish your machine had been working this weekend. We could have had quite a juicy conversation . . ."

"I didn't do anything," Leedy said. "I just dropped Deanna off and waved goodbye."

"You should have stuck around for the action. Ted said Terry was livid."

"What did he do?" Leedy asked, holding her breath.

"He threw her out on her perfect little bum," Jo Anne said, folding her arms across her chest. "I'm sure he said it as nicely as humanly possible. Although I wish he had told her to get on her broom and *FLY AWAY!*"

Leedy's ears were ringing with this new information. "You mean, Terry does not . . . *like* . . . Krissy?" was all she could think to say.

"Of course not!" Jo Anne said, trying to keep her voice low. "Terry knows Krissy is only interested in furthering her career . . . even if it means destroying his reputation along the way! And my husband, God bless him, had the nerve to ask Terry why he didn't take Krissy up on her offer!"

Leedy looked toward Terry and saw that Krissy was still standing in the front of the room, none too happy. Suddenly, she didn't look so pretty. For the first time, Leedy realized there was a hard, brittle edge to her appearance.

Krissy glared at Terry, her face a mask of indignant anger. She was speaking to him, her hand waving toward Jo Anne and Leedy in the back of the room. She looked their way, glaring daggers at Leedy.

"What was Terry's answer to Ted's question?" Leedy whispered to Jo Anne.

Jo Anne's reply was drowned out by angry voices in the front of the classroom. Leedy and Jo Anne looked up and saw that Krissy had abandoned whispering tersely in Terry's ear in favor of a more direct approach.

"Good luck, Mr. Foster," Krissy snarled. It was the first time Krissy had said anything loud enough for Leedy to hear her. "You're going to need it by the time I get done with you! I'm going to file a complaint with the University about your sexual harassment!"

She gave Leedy one last angry glare, tossed her hair behind her and then stomped out of the classroom, not looking behind her.

Jo Anne watched the scene happily and gave Leedy a happy wink. "Ted told me that Terry said he tried to explain to Krissy that he was interested in someone else . . ." She left the sentence hanging in the air because Terry was now almost right next to them.

"I'd like to see her try," he said, walking right up to Leedy. He slipped her hand into his and squeezed it. "Now let's get out of here before someone asks me another question. And don't forget, you and I have to talk."

"Okay," Leedy said, squeezing his hand too. "We'll talk."

He smiled at her and pushed his hand through his mop

of curly hair. He was flustered from his confrontation with Krissy, but also relieved.

"Can we go now?" Jo Anne chided him. "Before any more young, pretty girls show up and file complaints against the faculty."

He glanced at Leedy and shrugged as if to apologize. "Jo Anne, all those pretty girls have finally gone home. Except for you two ladies, of course."

"Of course," Jo Anne said and poked him in the arm. "Now can we go?"

Leedy swallowed the lump in her throat and put the tape recorder into her bookbag. Her hands were shaking and it was all she could do to not throw her arms around Terry and weep. He slipped his hand gently on her back and she could feel a slight tremble to his touch.

"I'm ready. Are you?" he asked. All she could do was nod.

Chapter Fourteen

"I'm glad we are all finally together," Jo Anne said. "I'm so excited, I feel as if I'm about to explode!"

"Yeah," Terry said, glancing at Leedy. "I'm glad too. I've been wanting to talk to both you and Leedy." He led them into the hallway. Leedy walked beside him, still holding his hand. She didn't care what Jo Anne thought. She was all through playing hard-to-get.

"I've been wanting to talk with you too," she said.

"This is business," Jo Anne interjected. "You two will have plenty of time to talk about other matters after I say what I have to say."

"What's this about, Jo Anne?" Leedy asked, suddenly curious. "Do you need banking advice from Terry?"

"Oh, yes," she said. "I need lots of banking advice."

They took Leedy's Jeep to a nearby coffee shop and found a booth along the wall. Jo Anne sat down on one side of the booth and Leedy sat down on the other. Her heart skipped a beat when Terry slid into the seat next to her. She felt his hand softly take hers underneath the table and squeeze it. Just the feel of his touch made her heart melt.

She picked up her menu with her free hand and pretended to study it intently while Jo Anne and Terry did the same. The waitress came quickly, and they all ordered coffee and cheeseburgers.

"I know you're both wondering why I asked you here tonight," Jo Anne began. Leedy tried to focus her eyes on her friend, but the feel of Terry's hand wrapped over hers was too distracting. Jo Anne has something important to say, Leedy suddenly realized, taking in the bright pink flush on her cheeks and the way her voice sounded breathless and quick. She had thought Jo Anne might have been still worked up over the Krissy Montgomery scandal, but obviously it was something more. But his hand was holding tightly onto hers and he was sitting so close it was driving her crazy. She was finding it hard to concentrate on the business at hand.

"I wanted to talk to Leedy about an idea I have," Jo Anne finally began. "But first, I want to tell you both that I've been rehearsing this speech all weekend, so, please don't interrupt me until I'm finished. After that I'll entertain discussion of all of your questions and concerns."

"Okay," Leedy said. "We won't interrupt."

"That would be an interruption," Jo Anne said with a sigh. Scolded, Leedy gestured that her lips were zipped shut and the invisible key had been duly discarded. Jo Anne took a deep breath and began again. "Okay, then, here goes nothing . . . As you already are aware, Leedy, you and I have a great deal in common. To a remarkable degree really . . . we've talked about this extensively, right?"

"Yes," Leedy said, forgetting she was not allowed to speak.

"And even though I'm twenty years older than you, we have similar backgrounds. In fact, we have so much in common, we have almost identical likes and dislikes."

"Yes," Leedy said, smiling at her encouragingly.

"No talking! . . . We both have a background in restaurant management. We both love to cook except you're a trained chef and I'm more of a self-taught baker. In fact, if you think about it, our skills compliment each other."

"True," Terry offered. "And you both want to open a restaurant."

"Yes," Jo Anne said. "But let me finish . . . Where was I? Oh, yes. The restaurants that Leedy and I both envision are amazingly similar. As a matter of fact, you could safely say the restaurants we both have in mind are almost one and the same." Leedy nodded again and Jo Anne went on. "We both want an upscale, sophisticated restaurant that serves gourmet food. We both want a banquet hall and a wine cellar."

"And we've both failed to get loans," Leedy reminded her.

"Right," Jo Anne said. "And that's the problem."

"No kidding," Leedy said. "Now tell me something I don't know."

"You're not understanding me, Leedy," Jo Anne said. "The problem is as clear as the nose on our faces but we never stopped to think about it. Even now, you have hit the nail right on the head and still don't know it."

"I'm sorry," Leedy said, confused. "I'm not following you."

"Let me explain it again," Jo Anne said. "The problem

is that *both* of us have failed to make our restaurants a reality."

"Yes," Leedy said. "Don't rub it in. We've both failed to open our restaurants."

"Don't you see?" Jo Anne yelped, her voice rising in excitement. "You said it again! We *both* failed to get our loans approved. Think about it, Leedy! What if we tried to open up a restaurant *together*?"

"Huh?" Leedy asked. She suddenly forgot that Terry was still holding her hand underneath the table.

"Don't you get it?" Jo Anne continued. "Our problem is that both of us are trying to do this *alone*!"

Terry's face split into a huge smile. "I was hoping you two would come to this conclusion. I love it, Jo Anne! It's a great idea! And it just might work."

Leedy looked at Terry and then back to Jo Anne. "What idea?"

"You're not making this easy on me, are you?" Jo Anne exclaimed. "Earth to Leedy! Let's open a restaurant together! You and me. We can be partners!"

Leedy was not sure if she heard them right. "What?" she asked.

"We could do it!" Jo Anne exclaimed.

It took a minute for the words to sink in. Leedy had never considered sharing her dream of opening her own restaurant with anyone else. "Together?"

"Yes!" Jo Anne said, practically shouting. "We'll make terrific partners! Why not? We both want the same thing!"

It was an idea that made her head spin. A partnership? With Jo Anne? Jo Anne who knew enough about the business to manage ten restaurants. Jo Anne who tackled every problem with an energy that Leedy envied. Jo Anne who had become a dear friend.

"I never thought about a partnership," Leedy stammered. "It isn't a bad idea."

"I heard that the old bakery on the corner of seventh and Market Streets is available to buy," Terry said. "That might be just the place you two have been looking for."

"We could go look at it, Leedy," Jo Anne said. "What do you say?"

"I guess it couldn't hurt to look," she said, reeling.

"So, you will think about it?" Jo Anne asked, gleefully.

"Yes," Leedy said. "I'll think about it." It was an idea that had never occurred to her before, but now that the seed had been planted, she was starting to like it. Suddenly the idea of two people with the same dream working together seemed like the obvious solution to both of their problems.

Jo Anne reached across the table and squeezed her other hand. "I have a feeling this is the start of something great," she said, echoing Leedy's sentiments.

"We have lawyers at the bank who can help you put together a partnership agreement," Terry offered. "You will need to present a business plan, and a . . ."

"Stop talking like a banker, Terry!" Jo Anne warned. "I'm too excited to think about the business details. Right now, I just want to revel in my euphoria!"

"Okay, okay!" he laughed. "But Leedy hasn't agreed to anything yet. Give her a few days to get used to the idea. Then she will be able to make up her mind."

"She's already made up her mind," Jo Anne insisted. "I can tell. And we'll work out all of the details later." Leedy looked at Jo Anne and smiled. "This is it, kid!" Jo Anne gushed. "What you and I have both been working for! I know we can make it happen!"

The waitress set down the plates of food onto the table, but no one seemed hungry. Jo Anne was too excited about her business proposal and Leedy couldn't seem to take her eyes off Terry. The events of the evening had become too much to take in. First Krissy Montgomery was cast away, once and for all, then Jo Anne made her stunning proposition. And throughout it all, there was Terry. He was sitting close enough for her to feel his firm body next to hers and smell his fragrant masculine aroma. It was all too much for her to contemplate in one night.

Jo Anne's face broke into a smile and she suddenly stood up and stretched across the table so she could give Leedy an enormous hug. The position was an awkward one so Leedy had to let go of Terry's hand so that she could span the distance of the table and return the embrace.

She shut her eyes while they hugged and, suddenly, she could see the restaurant she had been dreaming of for so many years. The vision only lasted for a fleeting moment, but she could see it so clearly, she could almost touch it. There it was, in an old building with large windows all around. There were black shutters on the upper-level windows and a dark green canopy framed around the front door. Leedy knew, just from the outside, that this restaurant was hers. And she knew it was beautiful. It was grand and comfortable, elegant and sophisticated, all at the same time, and the food offered was the best in town. She could barely see herself standing inside the doorway. But she was not standing alone. In the doorway to her dream restaurant, Jo Anne was standing with her. They were both smiling and waving, welcoming in the hungry patrons. It was a wonderful sight, Leedy and Jo Anne together in the doorway of this grand restaurant. Standing side by side, working to make their dream come true.

She returned the hug with an enthusiasm that came from deep inside her. This was the moment when Leedy and Jo Anne became partners. A union formed by necessity and sealed with an embrace between friends.

Jo Anne pulled away, wiping a tear from her eye. "I'm so excited!" she gushed. "This went much better than I dared to expect." Terry pulled a handkerchief from his pocket and handed it to her. She softly wiped her eyes, clutching the soft white cotton as tears spilled down her cheeks. Then they sat down to talk about the restaurant that would come to be while they ate their cheeseburgers.

They were sipping a second cup of coffee when Jo Anne suddenly jumped to her feet. "This has been the best night of my life," she said. "Well, almost the best . . . I'm not that pathetic! But if you two don't mind, I'm going to go home and tell my husband the good news."

She pulled on her coat and grabbed her purse before Terry barely had a chance to get to his feet. "Stay for dessert?" he offered.

"And keep you two dunderheads from finally talking to each other alone?" Jo Anne exclaimed. "Not a chance!"

Leedy gazed at Terry pensively and saw that he was smiling gratefully at Jo Anne. "Thanks," he said, helping her on with her coat. He kissed her on the cheek and gave her a hug. "I'll call you in the morning and let you know the time of the first of many meetings."

"No, Terry," Jo Anne said, grabbing him around the neck and planting a sloppy wet kiss on his check. "Thank you! You have been wonderful! Neither Leedy nor I could have

come this far without your help. And, if we somehow manage to get this thing up and going, you're the one who has
made it all possible."

"Shut up," Terry said, grinning. "I did not do any such
thing. You two are the most resourceful women I've ever
met. You each would have made your restaurant eventually.
I didn't do anything but teach my stupid class."

"That's not the way I see it," Jo Anne said, grinning.
"The three of us are a team now, Terry. I can feel it in my
bones! And we are going to do just fine with our one restaurant." With that, Jo Anne slapped Terry on his rear end,
gave Leedy a bawdy wink and took off out the door before
another word could be said.

"I don't know what to say," she told Terry. "I feel happy
and confused and overwhelmed . . . all at the same time."

"Do you like the idea?" he asked. "Because if you feel
the slightest bit of apprehension, you should put it out on
the table now."

"It's not that," she said. "I think Jo Anne and I will make
a wonderful team. We'll work through any snags that might
come up. I know it won't be easy, but we're both smart,
savvy women who understand the restaurant business.
Right? Naiveté was never the problem for either of us. No,
I think Jo Anne and I will build a great restaurant together.
And it will be successful too. Heaven knows, we both have
worked hard to get it."

"That's true."

"And we want the same thing. The motivation is there
for both of us."

"And you both are blessed with similar easygoing per-
sonalities," Terry pointed out. "If you should happen to

disagree on something, you'll both be willing to sit down and discuss it."

Leedy cocked her head to one side. "Right," she said. "It's not like I would run out of anyone's office in tears or anything."

"That was before," he said. "You've changed since then."

"I have, have I?" she noticed the grin on his face. "Don't be so sure of that," she warned. "I could cry at the drop of a hat."

"No," he said. "It was only one little teardrop, and it's okay to be human. Take your time and think this over before you give Jo Anne an answer. It is your decision and only your decision. Don't rush into any business arrangement until you have considered every pitfall."

"Don't worry," she said. "I will. But, Jo Anne was right when she said I had already made up my mind. I have."

"You have?"

"Yes," Leedy said. "Or rather, let's just say my mind is ninety-eight percent made up."

"You're that certain?"

"Yes. I don't know why, but as soon as Jo Anne said it, I knew it was a great idea. I can't explain it, but I have a good feeling about this."

"I can't explain it either," Terry said. "But I do too . . . And I'm notoriously cautious about recommending business partnerships. However, in this case, it just makes good sense."

They sat there next to each other in the close booth, despite the recent vacancy in the seat across from them, and looked at each other. Leedy suddenly became very aware of the proximity between them. She could feel him, barely touching her body with his, and for a moment she simply enjoyed the closeness of his body. Neither one spoke.

She swallowed and took a deep breath. "Look," she said and winced at the sound of her shaking voice. "I . . . um . . . There's something I have been meaning to ask you."

"What is it?" he asked.

Leedy was determined to say what she had to say before she chickened out. "Do you remember my friend from Mr. Hobo's? Brittany?"

"Yes," he said. "Cute blonde girl, right? She's the one getting married?"

"Yes," she said. "As a matter of fact, her wedding is next Saturday and I was wondering if . . . I know this is short notice . . . But I was wondering if you . . ."

"I would love to," he said. His voice was low and sexy and he was almost whispering in her ear.

"But you don't know what I was going to ask you yet," she said.

"Were you going to ask me to escort you to your friend's wedding?" he asked.

"Yes. I mean . . . if you're not too busy, that is."

"Then, I would love to go," he said again.

"Are you sure?" she said. "Isn't Deanna coming home for the weekend? I don't want to mess up your plans. I was going to ask you last week, after class, but . . ."

"But Krissy was there?" he asked, finishing Leedy's sentence. Her face flushed and she nodded.

"Are you seeing her?" she asked. She knew she had no right to ask, but she had to hear the truth from him about his relationship with Krissy. No matter what it might be.

Terry softly took her by the hand. "I wanted to talk to

you after class last week too," he began. "But Krissy asked for a ride to the garage, and . . ."

She looked into his eyes and she saw the familiar expression again. The expression of yearning and passion. It was a look of longing that made her forget all about Krissy Montgomery.

"Leedy, you have nothing to worry about with Krissy," he said. "I never had any interest in her whatsoever. I've been wanting to tell you that for weeks, but . . ."

"But what?" she asked.

"But you were so dedicated to your restaurant," Terry admitted. "And you were afraid of what people would think if we were together. Not that I care about what people think . . ." His hand tightened on hers and he looked at her mournfully. "It is just that I was not sure if you had room in your career plans for a monkey wrench like me." He was looking into her eyes, drinking her up.

Leedy felt her insides ache with desire as she melted into his arms.

"You wouldn't be a monkey wrench in my plans," she said, her voice quivering. "As a matter of fact, you would be helpful. Um . . . Jo Anne and I may need some help filling out all the forms and . . . paperwork. You know all about financial paperwork, right?"

Terry slid closer to her, a soft smile playing on his lips. "Yes. I know all about forms. I can help you and Jo Anne with the loan application," he said softly. "The Approval Committee meets next week. If we work quickly, we can get the application to them by then."

"Okay," Leedy said, breathlessly. He was so close she could feel his warm breath and smell his aftershave. Terry looked into her eyes.

"I'll help you . . ." he murmured, his voice low. He reached out and gently touched her chin, caressing it softly. "I'm sure we can hammer out all the details," he whispered, just before he kissed her.

His mouth closed over hers, deliciously soft and warm. Leedy returned the kiss with an urgency that surprised her. It was as if she had been waiting for his kiss for almost as long as she had been dreaming of her restaurant. His tongue hungrily found hers and she felt as if she would explode with yearning.

"I've been wanting to kiss you again ever since that first time," he whispered.

"Oh?" she said dumbly, her head in a fog of passion.

"Yes," he said. "I've wanted to kiss you since the moment I laid eyes on you. Ever since the day you walked into my office." His mouth found hers again and they kissed for a long, burning moment. "I think about you all the time. I can't eat. I can't sleep. I can't think of anything but you." He kissed her again, his mouth moving down to her neck.

"Ahem," a voice said from above them. Leedy and Terry looked up and saw the waitress standing at the table next to them, a wide grin on her face. "Can I get you two anything else?" she asked. "More coffee? Some dessert? Or maybe you're ready for the check?"

His face reddened. "Just the check, please," he said and Leedy broke into embarrassed giggles. He looked at her and then he began laughing too.

"We should learn to use some self-control when we're out together in public," he said, kissing her again.

"I don't know," she said, holding him tightly. "This way is kind of fun too."

Chapter Fifteen

The old bakery building on the corner of Seventh and Market Streets was more spectacular than either Jo Anne or Leedy expected. The two-story structure was made of weathered grey stones, and it sat far back from the street, but not so far as to be hidden. Although it was more than one hundred years old, the previous owners had renovated it in all the important places while not disturbing the building's timeless beauty. The corner building was blessed with large front windows that overlooked the bustling main street of downtown Madison.

"We could put an awning up over the doorway," Jo Anne said.

"A big, black awning, like at Nickoby's," Leedy added. "Perfect."

"And maybe a green canopy for the front of the door."

"Great idea," Jo Anne said

"I think there's enough room for a dining area outside

when the weather is nice. On the side facing Market Street perhaps."

"We could put up some wrought iron rails to mark off the dining section," Jo Anne said. "If we keep the area narrow and we use both sides of the building, there should be plenty of room for at least eight or nine tables."

"That will work," Leedy said thoughtfully. "It was nice of the agent to give us the key. I'm glad we have the chance to look at the place by ourselves."

"It was not nice of her," Jo Anne corrected. "She already has two other buyers interested in this building. She knows she will have a contract by the end of the day no matter what. So why waste her time personally showing it?"

"Two other buyers?" Leedy asked, her heart sinking. "Do we have a chance?"

"I think so," Jo Anne said. "Terry says we have to act fast. He says the real estate firm owes him a favor, too. But we still have to make the best offer."

"This building does not look this big from the outside," Leedy remarked, swinging open the door into the dark and empty building.

Jo Anne led the way through the front room, snapping on lights as she went along. "We'll need to knock down some walls to make room for a big dining room. And that old storage area could be made into a banquet room. It looks as if it's plenty big enough."

The women worked their way quickly through to the back of the bakery. To the room they both wanted to see most.

"Thank goodness," Jo Anne said.

"They've modernized it," Leedy said, finishing her

thought. They walked through the kitchen, pulling open cabinets and looking into drawers.

"I think these ovens will do just fine," Leedy said. "I'm happy to see they're gas. And it's a good thing too. Have you seen the prices the new commercial ovens are going for these days?"

"They're through the roof," Jo Anne agreed. "I hope these have not been sitting for too long. They don't appear to be that old. We certainly aren't lacking for oven space. There are, what, a half-dozen double ovens in this kitchen. We may need another cook top though." They opened and shut more drawers and cabinets and lingered in the enormous kitchen.

"Probably," Leedy remarked. "And the floors need some work."

"The real estate broker said there is hardwood underneath the industrial-duty olive green carpeting in the lobby area, but the kitchen floor is another matter."

"It looks as if it's been painted with a high-gloss paint." Leedy examined the chipped, worn red paint that covered the kitchen floor. "I bet it could get pretty slippery when it's wet," she noted. "Maybe some black and white no-skid commercial-grade floor tiles might work out for us. We should research the facts first though."

"I like the stainless steel cabinets," Jo Anne commented. "After a good scrubbing, they will be fine. Shoot, we could get my boys in here and they'll have it clean as a whistle in no time. We'd have to cough up a few bucks though. But, don't worry, they work cheap."

"This place is perfect," Jo Anne said and Leedy agreed.

"The square footage is enormous!"

"Bigger than either of us had hoped for."

"We'll need to hire an architect to remodel the floor plan. And the bathroom facilities could use a facelift."

"Terry already has scheduled a meeting for us with an architect," Jo Anne said.

"He's that confident we'll get the loan?" Leedy asked.

Jo Anne shrugged. "I don't know. All he said was this architect was booked solid for the next year, but he's the best in town and he has agreed to work with us. Another favor he called in on our behalf."

"The location is perfect," Leedy mused. "We won't have any problems getting people to notice us. It will be ideal for romantic dates, homecoming parties, weddings . . ."

"And being on the corner gives it a strong curb appeal," Jo Anne added, imitating Terry's classroom voice perfectly. Leedy giggled.

"Speaking of the infamous professor," Jo Anne said. "How goes it with Mr. Foster?"

"Fine," Leedy said, with a twinkle in her eye. "As a matter of fact, the last time I saw him he seemed like the happiest man in town." It was all she could do to keep from swooning like a love-struck schoolgirl.

"Have you seen him lately?"

"We went to lunch yesterday," Leedy said.

"More smooching in public places?" Jo Anne asked.

"A little, but we're trying to keep it G-rated."

"How is Deanna taking this new and improved Uncle Terry?"

"She's happy for us," Leedy said.

"She isn't putting you through her boot camp?" Jo Anne asked, surprised.

"No."

"No whipped cream in your purse or thumbtacks on your chair?"

"Of course not!" Leedy said. "Deanna is my friend."

"You're luckier than any of the others," Jo Anne noted. "Not that there were that many. I guess since she had already given you her blessing, she's not going to change her mind now. Once Deanna makes up her mind she likes someone, she'll be true blue."

"We went shoe shopping again last night," Leedy said. "She called up out of the blue and said that Terry suggested she call me. It sounded like fun to me, so we went. She bought a pair of bright yellow bowling shoes."

"They sound lovely."

"I got a pair in red," Leedy added. "They feel like a dream."

"I'm glad to hear you and Deanna have something in common," Jo Anne added. "Has Terry said anything about the loan?"

"No," Leedy said. "Terry and I have an agreement. I don't ask him about the loan and he doesn't question my champagne taste in restaurant decor."

"I'm not worried about it," Jo Anne said. "Terry Foster is a professional, through and through. As demonstrated by his telling Krissy Montgomery to take a hike."

"Oh, yes," Leedy said. "My old friend Krissy. Whatever happened to her?"

"I hear she signed up for Intermediate Small Business Management. It's on Tuesday and Thursday nights, and . . . it's taught by a lawyer from Schumaker & Jacoby—I think his name is Gregory Barlow—the poor dear."

Leedy giggled. She didn't mean to be catty, but it was a good feeling to know that Krissy was finally out of the picture. "I hope it all works out for her," Leedy said. "And for Gregory Barlow."

The women laughed and talked as they toured the former bakery. Both women were thinking of the potential of the space and neither of them wanted to leave, but they also knew they had to move quickly with an offer.

"I can't believe we are going to *buy* property," Leedy said. "I always thought I would lease space."

"It will be a good investment," Jo Anne said. "That is, if we make the best bid. Speaking of which, we better get back."

"I know," Leedy sighed. "I have to work late this afternoon. Although I'm finding it difficult to keep my mind on my job lately."

"Because of the restaurant or because of your sizzling love life?"

"Both," Leedy said, winking at her with a devilish grin. "But enough about me. Come on, partner. Let's go make an offer on this space before someone beats us to it."

"We can call the real estate agent from my cell phone," Jo Anne offered.

Jo Anne led the way to the door and Leedy followed close behind her. She hoped the seller accepted their bid. There was something about the place that felt comfortable, as if it already belonged to them. She took one last look around before she clicked off the light. "Our restaurant," she whispered to herself. "Our lifelong dream."

Chapter Sixteen

It was a beautiful day for a wedding. The sun was just beginning to set, and the sky was a lovely shade of blue intermixed with tints of purple, pink, and yellow. Terry and Leedy arrived at the church in a festive mood. It had been an exciting week and she was happy just to be with him. But it was also Brittany's big day—and a wedding. Leedy loved weddings. Something about the magnificence of a man and a woman walking down the aisle always made her feel so happy she wanted to cry. In fact, just the sound of the organ music was enough to bring tears to her eyes.

She had bought a new dress for the occasion months ago. It was a fitted, delicately smooth silk dress in a deep plum color that complimented Leedy's lustrous glossy dark hair. She had spent nearly a half-hour trying to coax her long tresses into a loose but secure bun, but she ended up with a slightly tousled, yet elegant, French twist.

"It isn't right," Terry told her when he arrived at her apartment to pick her up.

"What isn't right?" she asked, smoothing the silky material of her dress.

"You," he said. "You aren't supposed to be more beautiful than the bride."

"I beg your pardon?"

"You're gorgeous," he said and his eyes told her he meant it.

And Leedy felt gorgeous too. In fact, when Terry slipped his arm around her waist and led her out the front door, she had never felt so beautiful and so adored in her life. He led her to his Corvette and opened the car door for her. He climbed in behind the steering wheel and started the engine, barely able to keep his eyes off her. "Would you like me to put down the roof this time? Or would arriving at the wedding frozen be a faux pas?"

"No roof," Leedy told him. "One ill-timed gust of wind and my hair-do will self-destruct."

"I wouldn't want that to happen."

"Thank you, kind sir."

"This is going to be a wonderful evening," he said. "But it is dangerously close to being classified as a real date. What will people say?"

"I'm not worried about that anymore," she said. "The class is finished, and my loan application it sitting on Mrs. Jefferson's desk, remember?"

"So it is," he said, starting the engine. He had a wicked grin on his face as he winked at her. "So it is."

Once at the church, she sighed contentedly as he parked the car in the parking lot of the church. It had been a hectic week, what with all the paperwork, meetings with accountants and lawyers, and the endless contract negotiations. It was liberating to finally be able to slow down and relax, even if it was for just a short time. Leedy planned to enjoy watching Brittany and Mark take their wedding vows. And she planned to enjoy the company of Terry Foster even more.

The small church was charming. The gathering was just the right number of people—not too many, not too few, as Brittany had told her wistfully. It was shaping up to be a perfect day. In fact, Leedy couldn't remember the last time she had felt so certain and happy about her life. She looked up at Terry and smiled.

"Have I mentioned lately that you're gorgeous?" he said and slipped her hand into his.

The pews had been decorated with sprays of beautiful flowers, and she inhaled the intoxicating aroma as she was escorted to her seat. It was just as lovely inside the church as it had been outside. So much so, she could already feel her eyes start to smart.

The organ music was playing, but not the wedding march as yet. She could feel the sense of anticipation in the air as an elegantly dressed woman was being led to her seat by one of the handsome young ushers.

"I think that's Mark's mother," Leedy whispered. "She has the same red hair as Mark and Brittany told me she was wearing an ivory-colored satin and lace gown."

"She looks pleased to be here," Terry noted. "That's always a good sign."

Leedy elbowed him in the ribs. "Behave yourself," she warned. Another woman was being led down the aisle by a handsome young man. She was a tall, attractive woman with an elegant gown. "I think this woman is Brittany's mother, but I'm not sure. The usher is Chris. He's Brittany's brother. He's stopped by Mr. Hobo's a few times to visit her. He's a student at the University . . . a mechanical engineering major, I think. I know he's there on a tennis scholarship."

"What year is he in?" Terry asked, eyeing Chris suspiciously.

"Freshman, I believe," she replied. Then, suddenly, something clicked in Leedy's head. The blond hair, the tennis scholarship, the *name!* "Terry," she gasped. "I think Brittany's brother is a, um, friend of Deanna's!"

"Really?" Terry asked. "She has mentioned some boy named Chris once or twice, usually with this glazed look in her eye. Are you sure?"

"Maybe. I wonder if he's an astronomy buff."

"I can see the family resemblance," Terry said. "If this is the Chris I think it is, he's the boy she's dating. I wonder why he didn't invite Deanna to the wedding." Leedy was wondering the same thing herself, but she said nothing.

"The woman has to be Brittany's mother," Terry said. "They're all tall with blond hair."

"Yes. I think you're right. She's lovely . . . and that dress is stunning."

Chris led the woman to the front pew on the bride's side, kissed her on the cheek. He then strode back to the entrance of the chapel. The wedding party had begun to line up and Leedy saw the minister, groom, and best man take their places at the front of the church.

The wedding party entered the chapel, the bridesmaids proceeding first. They were dressed in identical, tea-length creamy ivory-colored gowns. The gowns were silk with a fitted bodice, the skirt flowing softly around their legs. They carried bouquets of charming yellow roses.

The matron of honor followed the bridesmaids. This was

Brittany's older sister, Jane. Her gown was similar to the others, but there was more detail around the neckline and hem. She was stunning, and there were tears in her eyes.

Following closely behind Jane was her three-year-old daughter, Elena. Next to Elena was Jane's son, six-year-old Michael. Michael held Elena's hand, firmly but gently, as he led her down the aisle, carefully watching his mother for cues. Elena carried a basket filled with red rose petals and, every step or so, would grab a handful of petals and toss them onto the floor. Michael clutched his ring bearer's pillow and mugged for the adoring audience.

Just then the organ music began to play the wedding march. Everyone turned to watch as Brittany walked down the aisle, holding tightly onto the arm of her proud father. Brittany wore a long, body-hugging silk gown in the perfect shade of ivory. In her arms, she carried a large bouquet of red roses that cascaded down the front of her dress. A veil covered her face, but Leedy could see that Brittany's eyes were focused on Mark who was standing at the altar waiting for her, his face a mixture of terror, determination, and love.

Brittany slowly walked down the aisle, taking slow controlled steps as she pulled her father along. She paused for a second when she passed Leedy and gave her a joyous smile. Leedy smiled back and gave her a thumbs up. When Brittany and her father finally reached the altar, her father turned her over to Mark, who quickly stepped forward. Brittany's father shook Mark's hand, kissed his daughter on the cheek, and then joined his wife in the front pew. The bride turned and faced the groom and he took her hand and squeezed it lovingly.

"Dearly beloved," the minister began. "We are gathered

here today to join these two young people, Brittany Nicole Richards and Mark Thomas Ellis, into the glorious bonds of holy matrimony . . ."

Leedy brushed away a tear and looked at Terry to see if he noticed. But he didn't mind that she was crying. He only smiled reassuringly and squeezed her hand.

". . . I'll digress for just a moment," the minister was saying, "to say that I've known Brittany since she was a child. And I've known Mark for several years as well. They're intelligent, ambitious, attractive young people. I'm honored to be here today for them. I'm also happy to be a witness to this blessed event. For you see, this couple—or should I say these intelligent, ambitious, attractive young people, are blessed in the way God wants his children to be blessed. Because Brittany and Mark are deeply in love. I'm here today for the same reason you're here today. We are here together to witness and celebrate the first moments of Brittany and Mark's new life together. And what glorious, blessed lives they will see."

Leedy felt a lump in her throat and she could no longer stop the tears from spilling down her cheeks. It was so beautiful. "I know, I know," Terry whispered. "I feel the exact same way. What her father must be paying for all this . . ." Then he put his arm around her waist and hugged her tenderly. But underneath the softness of his touch, Leedy felt something else. A tremble to his fingertips that told her he too, was moved.

"Do you, Mark Thomas Ellis, take this woman to be your lawfully wedded wife? To have and to hold from this day forward, for richer and poorer, in sickness and in health, as long as you both shall live?"

"I do."

"Do you, Brittany Nicole Richards, take this man to be your lawfully wedded husband? To have and to hold from this day forward, for richer and poorer, in sickness and in health, as long as you both shall live?"

"I do."

Leedy managed to pull herself together by the time Mark and Brittany walked back down the aisle, but it was a super-human effort. Only Terry's strong arm wrapped around her waist prevented her from bawling her eyes out, right there in the church. "Come along, Miss Collins," he said, leading her. "Let's go greet the newlyweds, shall we?"

He led her up the aisle. Out of necessity, he stood closely to her as they waited for the swarm of delighted wedding guests to make their exit. His hand was touching Leedy's back and she could feel the warmth and strength of his fingertips. Leedy felt a sudden dizzying warmth throughout her body that started in the depths of her being and spread until she felt tingly all over. "Are you all right?" Terry asked. "You look a little flushed."

"I'm fine," Leedy said, enjoying the soft, sexy intensity of his voice. He slipped his arm around her waist and led her out of the chapel. Leedy thought about skipping the reception, if only to have him all to herself that much sooner, but she knew Brittany would never understand. Or maybe she would.

The receiving line was long but the mood was so bois-terous, Leedy and Terry didn't mind the wait. "Lovely wed-ding," Terry said, shaking hands with Brittany's father when they finally were at the head of the line.

"Beautiful," Leedy added.

There was much hand-shaking and slaps on the back,

until Leedy and Terry found themselves standing in front of Chris.

"You did a splendid job," Leedy said, and hugged him. "Congratulations!"

"Thank you," Chris said. He was watching Leedy and Terry with a keen interest.

"Beautiful wedding," Terry said, shaking Chris' hand. "You're a friend of my niece, right? Her name is Deanna McQuinn?"

"Yes," Chris said. From the look on his face, Leedy realized the boy was startled. "I wasn't sure if Deanna had mentioned me to you. I'm Chris. Chris Richards. As a matter of fact, I invited Deanna to be here tonight. But she—"

"But she thought I would drop to the floor in a faint?" Terry asked.

"No. What Deanna described was closer to some kind of crazed, homicidal rampage."

"I see," Terry said, shaking his head thoughtfully. He waited a moment before speaking again. "You know, Chris, that's nonsense."

Chris' young face broke into a relieved grin. "That was exactly what I tried to tell Deanna! But she thought you would have a cow or something."

"When you get home tonight, please call Deanna and tell her that you have been formally invited to our house tomorrow," Terry said. "We can all go to a movie and grab a bite of dinner and clear up this whole misunderstanding."

"Thank you," Chris said, shaking Terry's hand again. "I'd like that, sir."

"Say about six o'clock?" Terry asked.

"Six o'clock is fine. We'll see you then."

Terry led Leedy out of the church and they breathed the cold evening air. "Ready?" he asked, taking her hand.

"Ready," Leedy said, and she was. Ready for anything. He led her to his Corvette and opened the door.

"I wish we could take down the roof," Terry commented. "I like the look you get in your eye when Susie hits eighty. But it is too cold for that tonight and I don't want to mess up your beautiful hair. At least not yet anyway."

"Oh?" she said, smiling coyly.

"Not yet," he said, flashing her his perfect smile. "As for later, I can't make any guarantees."

They kissed in the car. Ordinarily Leedy would have never considered taking part in such sophomoric, giddy behavior, but it felt more like stealing sweet, wonderful kisses than acting like love-struck teenagers. Smooching in the car, she sighed. Wouldn't Brittany be pleased?

The reception was in full swing by the time they arrived at the banquet hall. Leedy made a mental note to recheck the dimensions of the back room of what had once been the bakery's storage room. Maybe thinking about the restaurant would make her forget about the aching need that had developed in the pit of her stomach. A need only Terry could fulfill. She already knew the dimensions of the old bakery's storage room. She already knew that the Ryan-Riley Inn's banquet hall would be much larger than the hotel's reception hall, but rechecking details is what Leedy did best. She pulled out a worn pad of paper from her purse and flipped through the pages. Yes, she thought looking over the crowded room. Their banquet room was bigger.

The hall was decorated in a lovely shade of creamy yellow. A color that was tastefully used in the starched linen tablecloths and in the helium balloons that had been arched over the doorway. At the head of the room was a long banquet table set for the wedding party. Off to the side, a band played jazz music on a bandstand that stood before a small dance floor. The rest of the room was filled with large round tables covered with more crisply starched linen tablecloths. Each table held a gigantic centerpiece of white roses.

"We are at Table Number Eight," Terry said, holding up the small white card that had been laid out on a table when they entered the hall. He took Leedy's hand and led her through the crowded room. They passed Tables One through Seven without any difficulty and then found Table Nine.

"Okay," he said. "Here is Table Ten and Table Eleven."

"Table Twelve and Fourteen," Leedy said, confused. "There is no Table Thirteen either."

"Here is Fifteen and Sixteen," Terry looked as baffled as she did when he spotted a small table in the corner. "What is this?" he asked, leading her to the farthest corner of the room. "This is it," he said, perplexed. "Table Eight."

Leedy looked at the little white card in the center of the table that proclaimed the table to indeed be Table Number Eight but it was a much smaller table than the others. Leedy and Terry looked at each other, both with puzzled expressions on their faces. Table Eight, unlike all the other tables, was a table set for only two. And instead of the pale yellow linens that adorned all the other tables, the tablecloth was a deep emerald green, Leedy's favorite color. Also, the vases on the other tables held sprays of white roses. The vase on this table held a single red rose.

"This is cozy," Terry said, smiling. He pulled a chair out for her. "Maybe they ran out of room at the big tables."

"It really doesn't work that way," Leedy told him, mystified. "They would have worked us in with the others somehow."

"What then?"

"I think I smell a rat."

"Hello," a waiter said, bringing them crystal wine glasses and a bottle of white wine. "You must be Leedy and Terry?"

"Yes, we are," Terry said, the perplexed expression returning to his face.

"I've been expecting you," the waiter said. "I'm Bradley and I'll be your server this evening."

"Hi Bradley," Leedy said. "How come we're not at the big tables with everyone else?"

"Not that we're complaining," Terry added.

"We were wondering the same thing ourselves," Bradley told them. "But, I can assure you, this is no mistake. This was by special request from the bride herself. Mrs. Ellis wanted you two to have a table all to yourselves." He smiled broadly and poured white wine into their glasses. "But don't worry. I will not forget about you. As a matter of fact, you're my only table. I'll personally see to it that you have a wonderful time." Bradley poured them each a glass of wine, bowed, then disappeared back into the crowd of guests.

"That brat!" Leedy said to Terry after the waiter had left. "Brittany set this whole thing up!"

"I don't mind," he said, leaning toward her. "In fact, I think I might donate another place setting of that china she picked out. This is the best seat in the house. And the best seating arrangement I've ever seen at a wedding."

Leedy blushed, but she too thought it was the best seat

in the house and the best seating arrangement she had ever seen at a wedding. She sipped from her glass of wine and smiled up at him. "I guess I can live with it," she said.

They listened to the jazz music and talked, neither one having any desire to mingle with the crowd. The company of each other was enough for them. Suddenly, the room became loud and an excited buzz swept across the room.

"Ladies and gentlemen," the band leader said into the microphone. "May I present to you, for the very first time, Mr. and Mrs. Mark Ellis!"

The room went wild when Brittany and Mark swept into the room, making a grand entrance to the roaring applause of the approving crowd. Leedy tried to catch Brittany's eye, if only to stick out her tongue, but to no avail. It was obvious the bride had other things to attend to, what with greeting her guests, dancing with the groom and looking radiant. Leedy decided she would thank Brittany later.

Bradley was true to his word: he didn't forget about Table Eight. Terry and Leedy drank the good wine and enjoyed a delicious dinner. But the filet mignon didn't take her attention away from the handsome man who was sitting next to her. As a matter of fact, with each passing moment her thoughts increasingly turned to the tantalizing possibility that he might kiss her again. Leedy could almost imagine what his body would feel like next to hers. She closed her eyes and let the desire wash over her. She could hardly wait to feel his arms wrapped around her.

"Would you like to dance?" he asked, as if he was reading her mind. She nodded and he softly slipped his arm around her waist and led her to the dance floor.

She couldn't remember the last time she had gone dancing—it seemed like forever. Dancing was something Leedy loved dearly but rarely was able to do. For a fleeting second Leedy remembered how much Brian disliked dancing. It was then she realized that this was the first time since the breakup that she had thought about Brian and not felt sad. It was liberating to no longer feel sad about her ex-boyfriend. There was no sorrow and no regrets. In fact, she thought about Brian and his new fiancée and wished them both happiness. Things were not meant to work out between her and Brian. Both of them were meant for someone else.

Terry led her across the floor, and they danced as gracefully as a couple who had danced every day of their lives. They moved to the steady beat of the music, their bodies in perfect rhythm to each other. They danced to everything the band played. From pop to jazz to the Electric Slide and even the Chicken Dance. They danced until they were out of breath and thirsty and longing for their cozy table for two in the corner.

"Hey, you two," Brittany said, sliding up next to them on the dance floor. "Are you having fun?"

Terry gave Brittany an affectionate kiss of the cheek and shook Mark's hand.

Leedy gave Brittany a gigantic hug. "You're the most beautiful bride I've ever seen," she whispered in Brittany's ear. "And I owe you one."

"Yes, you do," Brittany said, returning the embrace. Then she turned her attention to Terry. "Isn't Leedy pretty?" she asked him, grinning her pixie's smile.

"Yes, she is," he said, smiling gratefully.

"We have to keep moving," Brittany said, hugging Leedy again. "We want to say hello to everyone and not all of our guests are as easily entertained as you two."

"We'll talk more later," Leedy promised as Brittany and Mark waved goodbye.

"Maybe we can all get together for dinner?" Brittany suggested. "After we get back from the honeymoon, of course."

"That sounds terrific," Leedy said. "You two have fun!"

"You too," Brittany called.

Terry led Leedy back to their table. "That was fun," he said. "You're a great dancer."

"You too!"

"We'll have to do this more often then," he said.

"I'm game, if you are."

"Oh, I'm game."

They sat down and he scooted his chair closer. "Would you like to go to a movie with me and Deanna tomorrow?" he asked. "And, of course, my new friend, Chris?" ·

"Yes," Leedy said. "Are you sure Deanna will not mind me tagging along?"

"Of course not," he said. "She wouldn't mind a bit. She doesn't know about Chris yet, but it was her idea to invite you. In fact, she was insistent."

"Okay then," Leedy said. "I would love to go."

"It is our Sunday tradition," he said. "But Deanna gets to pick out the movie, I'm afraid. She told me this rule isn't open to negotiation. Something about some obscure Wisconsin child protection law. I find it's best not to argue."

"I can see that," Leedy agreed.

"I must warn you though, her movies usually involve a lot of gun play and exploding oil tankers. I hope you didn't have something more romantic in mind."

Leedy grimaced. "I hate chick movies," she said.

"You do?" Terry said in mock surprise. "You're beautiful, smart, and you hate chick movies! Where have you been all my life?"

"Here and there," she said, smiling.

"So you will join us?"

"It sounds like fun," she said.

"I'll pick you up at five, and we'll go back to my place and wait for the kids."

Bradley appeared and refilled their wine glasses. He was true to his word. He took care of their every need, but they barely noticed he was there.

"Remind me to offer him a job," Leedy said, clinking her glass with Terry's.

"I will," he said. "In fact, that brings up something I've been wanting to tell you all night."

"What's that?" she asked, enjoying the taste of the good Chardonnay.

"I was going to wait until Monday when we could have Jo Anne with us, but . . ."

"What is it?" Leedy asked.

"I shouldn't say."

"Oh, come on. You brought it up!"

"All right," he said, holding back his excitement. "I'm going to explode if I don't tell you. Are you ready?"

"Yes!"

"Your loan application was approved," he said, his face breaking into a huge grin. "The approval committee met last night. The director called me this morning and told me."

For a second, Leedy sat staring at Terry as if she had not heard what he had said. "What did you say?" she finally asked.

He carefully repeated every word he had just said, but she was still unable to fully grasp the importance of the message.

"Are you sure?" she stammered, blinking.

"You heard me!" Terry exclaimed. "Leedy! Your loan was approved!"

She looked at him blankly, trying to comprehend the enormity of his announcement. "Say it again," she said. "Say it slower this time. I want to be sure I get every single word!"

"You, Miss Leedy Collins, along with your partner, have been approved for a small-business loan," he said. "You know. Remember? There was some mooning about a life-long dream of owning a restaurant? That loan?"

Leedy leaped up from her chair and screamed "Yahoo!" She threw her arms around him and squeezed him with all of her might, nearly knocking him off his seat, not caring that people seated at the tables nearby were looking at them curiously. "We did it!" she shouted, grabbing hold of his shoulders and shaking him. "We did it! We did it! We did it!"

"*You* did it," he said, jumping up with her. He wrapped her in his arms and twirled her in the air.

"You helped me!" she cried. "I couldn't have done it without you!"

"No," Terry said. "The only thing I did was give the Approval Committee my recommendation. They made the final decision to approve it. You did it, Leedy! You and Jo Anne."

"We couldn't have done it without you though," she repeated, hugging him tightly.

"It was the least I could do," he said. "I mean, after all, you're the woman I adore."

"You . . . adore me?"

"Yes," he said, the look of longing returned to his blue eyes. "I want to be a part of your lifelong dream, too, Leedy. Whatever it happens to be. I love you."

She looked at him, too happy to speak. The news about the restaurant was good, but the words coming from his lips were even better.

"Say it again," she said. "Only say it slower this time. I want to be sure I get every single word!"

"Leedy," Terry whispered, holding her close to him. "I'm madly in love with you. I have been since the first time I laid eyes on you. Ever since the day you walked into my life. You're beautiful and smart and exciting and I want to spend the rest of my life with you." He leaned forward and kissed her. "I love you," he whispered softly in her ear.

He kissed her again and she felt it all the way to her curled toes. "I love you too, Terry," she said, fighting back the tears of joy. He kissed her again, and again, his lips pressing against hers with an insistence that made her knees feel weak. Her mouth yielded to the delicious touch of his sweet kisses as her desire drove her deeper and deeper into his arms.

Suddenly the sound of applause was ringing in her ears and she reluctantly pulled away from him. Maybe it was time for Brittany and Mark to make a toast or something. Leedy looked up, instead to find that the entire reception hall was looking in their direction, applauding, hooting and cheering wildly. Leedy noticed Brittany standing next to

Mark, her eyebrows raised in mock horror, a victorious smile on her face.

"Maybe we should find a more private place to do our kissing," Leedy whispered in Terry's ear.

"You're right," he said, slipping his arm around her waist and facing them both out to bow for the crowd. "Maybe we should. And I just happen to know of the perfect place."